Another World

Also by Melvyn Bragg

FICTION
For Want of a Nail
The Second Inheritance

The Cumbrian Trilogy:
The Hired Man
A Place in England
Kingdom Come

The Nerve
A Christmas Child
Without a City Wall
The Silken Net
Autumn Manoeuvres
Love and Glory
Josh Lawton
The Maid of Buttermere
A Time to Dance
A Time to Dance: the screenplay
Crystal Rooms
Credo
The Soldier's Return
A Son of War
Crossing the Lines
Remember Me . . .
Grace and Mary
Now is the Time
Love Without End

NON-FICTION
Speak for England
Land of the Lakes
Laurence Olivier
Cumbria in Verse (edited)
Rich: The Life of Richard Burton
On Giants' Shoulders
The Adventure of English
12 Books that Changed the World
In Our Time
The South Bank Show: Final Cut
The Book of Books
William Tyndale: A Very Brief History
Back in the Day

Melvyn Bragg

Another World

The Oxford Years: A Memoir

Sceptre

First published in Great Britain in 2026 by Sceptre
An imprint of Hodder & Stoughton Limited
An Hachette UK company

The authorised representative in the EEA is Hachette Ireland, 8 Castlecourt Centre, Dublin 15, D15 XTP3, Ireland (email: info@hbgi.ie)

1

Copyright © Melvyn Bragg 2026

The right of Melvyn Bragg to be identified as the Author of the Work has been asserted by him in accordance with the Copyright, Designs and Patents Act 1988.

All rights reserved. No part of this publication may be reproduced, stored in a retrieval system, or transmitted, in any form or by any means without the prior written permission of the publisher, nor be otherwise circulated in any form of binding or cover other than that in which it is published and without a similar condition being imposed on the subsequent purchaser.

A CIP catalogue record for this title is available from the British Library

Hardback ISBN 9781399755429
ebook ISBN 9781399755436

Typeset in Sabon MT by Hewer Text UK Ltd, Edinburgh
Printed and bound in Great Britain by Clays Ltd, Elcograf S.p.A.

Hodder & Stoughton policy is to use papers that are natural, renewable and recyclable products and made from wood grown in sustainable forests. The logging and manufacturing processes are expected to conform to the environmental regulations of the country of origin.

Hodder & Stoughton Limited
Carmelite House
50 Victoria Embankment
London EC4Y 0DZ

www.sceptrebooks.co.uk

Dedicated to Julia Matheson, a good friend and colleague for more than fifty years

Preface

This book is a sequel to *Back in the Day*, a memoir set almost exclusively in my home town of Wigton during the first eighteen years of my life.

From there I went to Oxford University which I realised was not just an academic hothouse but a gateway to many unforeseen opportunities. This altered the structure and nature of the book. It became a succession of scenes from those years in which locations change and detailed digressions take centre stage as the story goes from the past to the present.

Part One

Chapter One

I followed the train moving hesitatingly on the long curve towards Wigton railway station as if it were reluctant to reach its destination.

The station was built on a classical model in local sandstone. The line started from Carlisle eleven miles to the east and swept through Wigton to the sea and down the rim of Cumbria, hugging the coast until it reached its destination of Barrow-in-Furness.

From the platform I could see across Wigton. The town nested in a shallow bowl before suddenly lifting up to the northern fells dominated by Skiddaw. There were three defining structures – the tall factory chimney next to the station sometimes seeping a rank smell into the town, St Mary's Church in the middle of the town and further south the eccentric Highmoor Tower, a mock Venetian structure jammed on top of a Georgian house. These landmarks seemed to tie together the auctions, the slaughterhouse, the covered market, the Norse High Street and its crofts, the network of small huddled houses, the pubs, the churches, chapels, schools and shops. Population about five thousand. I could close my eyes and walk through it – as I often did to get to sleep. Just above the station was a spot called Standingstone, the name and the stone indicating Stonehenge times.

Sarah and I had been out the previous night and agreed that she would not come to see me off. It would be too dramatic. I would be back in a few weeks. We would write. We had met at school in our early teens, myself two years the elder.

Then Sarah arrived! Of course she did. Took her dinner-hour break early from the bank, biked down to the station, and looked as embarrassed as I felt. It was great! It was like a movie. She gave me a letter.

We did not kiss on the platform. There were three other passengers waiting to travel. Sarah had guessed my mother would have done the sandwiches. So she brought a packet of dark chocolate digestive biscuits. We said very little to each other. The arrival of the train was a relief.

I leant out of the compartment window and waved. The awkward gesture was shyly returned. Sarah was not one for show. I can see her still. Long, thick black hair, complexion tanned over the seasons by weather, almost an hourglass figure that her working clothes could not entirely disguise. She was beautiful. Why was I leaving? We had just begun.

She stood there diminishing, immobile, until I could see her no longer.

* * *

I hurried up into the university city from the station, a suitcase in each hand, a rucksack sagging down my back. A sunny autumn afternoon, leaves still to fall, the streets more crowded than when I had come to take scholarship exams and students were on vacation, giving newcomers their accommodation and their chance. This busyness lent Oxford excitement.

Another World

From the two previous visits for exams I remembered a basic map. Twist to the left to pass Worcester College, just one of more than thirty colleges, this one with a full-size cricket pitch and a lake in the grounds. Effortless wealth and privilege everywhere. Turn right to pass between the Ashmolean Museum and the grand Randolph Hotel. On to the site of the Christian martyrs burnt alive for their faith, and into Broad Street which trickled out opposite the colleges into narrow alley and small shop tributaries, reminders of Wigton. There was the stern solidarity of Balliol College, Trinity College, Blackwell's famous bookshop and another hub: Christopher Wren's masterpiece, the Sheldonian Theatre.

Beyond that you could see the dome of the Radcliffe Camera library, squatting like the bald brain of the university next to the slim ornate spires, spears reaching to the sky from the exclusive scholarly college of All Souls. Left again to Wadham College. It was modest but classical, seventeenth century, plain, perfect. When I went through the gates I felt that I had arrived in an unthreatening place for work. Centuries of it built to outlast and reshape all who entered.

And there was the porter I remembered from the last time, smiling, waving me through the heavy doors. He offered to help with the suitcases but I held on to them. I was shown the array of alphabetically listed boxes in a side room where the mail would land. Staircase Two was pointed out, a key handed over. I was in. I bumped my way up the narrow staircase, using the suitcases as buffers.

The first quad was a square, everywhere the local fawn stone. At one end, facing the entrance, were the chapel and the Hall, joined as a single building. The sides of the quad were the rooms, mostly for pairs of undergraduates, except for the attics, enviably I thought, single. My mood hovered between excited and apprehensive. A suspicion that this was all a mistake. So many young men. So different from those I had left behind on the streets of Wigton. Another world, even a different species. Homo Sapiens to my Neanderthal.

The majority, it seemed at first sight, had known public school and were at ease in this continuation. There was that manner and the calm interiority, even a uniformity of facial expression, rather aloof. Or was that no more than a surface? The mood was distant but not unfriendly. To me, Oxford was a new landscape, populated by branded differences, not only the public school caste but those who had done their two years' National Service, fought in West Africa or Malaya or learned Russian in the Baltic. Adults. Already a life led. I was one of the minority who had not been called up for military service, a casualty – or beneficiary – of a change in government recruitment policy. It was, though, one of the factors in the geometry of class at the university at that post-war time, a time when the armed forces still reverberated importance and authority.

The university seemed to me like one uniform settlement. Oxford soon became a permanent floating island in my mind, intricately interconnected, one of a kind. Its unpretentious splendour was intertwined with cosiness, comfortable places, calm little landing stations. Built for study, serving privilege, sponging up knowledge. It was the buildings that capped it: you could scarcely go down a side street or turn a corner without being confronted by a past set in stone whose prime purpose over centuries had been to increase information, slake curiosity, discover the new, test the old, turn out an elite. Above all, largely a space for men. Another strange twist, foreign to those who had been schooled alongside girls and women.

It was the crowding of the colleges in the centre of the city that made it such an intriguing cat's cradle. This might seem near-preposterous, but in Oxford, the city, the streets, the sites and the sights, I soon felt the comfort I felt in wandering through the streets, multiple alleys, gimmels and unnamed yards of my home town of Wigton. There was the same experience – pleasure – in being in such a maze of a place. In Oxford the attraction was bonded with learning: in Wigton it was cemented in community. Whatever was at work, from the beginning, I felt that Oxford was as easy as your old shoe, unfailingly unique, its studious serenity long achieved and signed off, like the blessing at the close of Anglican evensong. By limiting itself to one constant aim it included everything. And the city itself was embraced by a coil of rivers, given lungs by parks and pastures, encircled by History, a miniature kingdom.

Just to walk the streets was to feel good. And if the black dog was biting, or when a fat thumb was pressing down on a brain-bruise, then all the more reason to go out and roam, just as I would embrace the open countryside of Cumbria and wait for the force of place to rub away the depression. Oxford's mellow-stoned labyrinth did that.

The university was seductive. It was not entirely unlike falling for someone, sewn into my immediate idealisation of the place.

It is still there in fresh memory, more than sixty years on, undiminished, a citadel of learning, a testament to what is good, perhaps what is unique about us – ceaseless curiosity, reaching out to know the answers to the ancient and modern questions that may never be solved, or rather like walking in the Lake District where you come, as you think, to the top of a fell, only to look ahead and see, waiting for you, another higher, unvisited fell – and welcome it.

* * *

The only previous occasions on which I had sat at long tables eating with scores of strangers was at Butlin's, Ayr, three years running in the early 1950s. The splendid Jacobean Hall at Wadham College worked on a similar principle: shovel them in, feed them up and usher them out. The key difference was that those who occupied the long, hard university benches were exclusively young men, row on row, black gowned, collar and tie, there for education not entertainment. At Butlin's we would follow Redcoats around the campsite in the evening singing, 'Please put a penny on the drum – we haven't got a tanner, to buy a new pianner, so please put a penny on the drum!' 'Come and join us! Come and join us!' we sang as we walked through that enchanted world. We entered the Hall for lunch and dinner at Wadham less exuberantly, but there was a resemblance. Butlin's was Oxford, the carnival.

At one end of the Hall was a minstrels' gallery, at the other, the long High Table, across the dining room, cutting short the advance of the undergraduate tables, all oak, all gleaming with polish. This top table hosted the tutors, the dons, the thought counsellors and their guests. Their high table was lit by tall candles, their food and drink superior.

Another World

On this first night of the new term in the new academic year I remember little of the conversation. Most of us had secured places there finally by the Interview. We were experienced in acceptable patter. A long Latin grace had introduced and styled the evening; beer was a lubricant; the college servants, known as scouts, served the young men (the word 'student' was not in the currency), a scene replicated in more than thirty other colleges in that largely mediaeval city. The form had scarcely loosened over eight centuries. Despite being foreign to it, I liked it from the start, not least because in whichever group you landed at the table, you soon became involved in a discussion which could feel significant in such a context. The challenge was to take on all subjects, whether you knew much or not. Participation was what mattered.

The inherited idea of the Oxford Man elbowed out the reality, which was that, like other colleges and universities all over the country, it was a forcing house for ambitious adolescents with some skills in memory, logical thought and learning. It specialised in a curriculum of teaching taken to be essential for class-one success. It was also a finishing school for those basking in a taste of the equivalent of the European tour. Most obviously it was an officers' training ground, for leaders in the Church, and, on an epic scale, positions in government, in the law, in high office, across the upper crust. We were made aware of this. We had been chosen by the traditional mechanism by those themselves so chosen before us . . . We had been slotted into a well-trodden process which held on to its eminence and gripped it fast.

After dinner there were dozens of second-year touts beckoning for new recruits for their clubs – history, rugby, choir, film, chess clubs, drama clubs, the Union. And the city sported a congregation of pubs, some of them more ancient than the colleges. There was no television in the College. There were cliques in the making. And the city itself to browse, to weave between the spires and the towers, the domes, the quiet, quaint alleys, the rich and rare shops, the immersive jigsaw. It seemed a foreign country, welcoming occupation.

Like many others, I'd guess, in those early days I strolled around smitten. Despite the good order and formality of the dinner there had been a fever about it. The surface gilt of nervous old custom and practice concealed a much more vigorous and demanding agenda. Like other newcomers, I'm sure, there was so much to take in that I needed to burst out.

I went across to Merton Lane which I had used for a similar dousing purpose when I came to Oxford to take the scholarship exams. Cobbled, narrow, studded with antique colleges which had produced radical learning and revolutionary action in their day, but at this mid-century, mid-evening time, seemingly perfect and at peace. Lit by rather dim lamplight, the cobbles gleamed from recent rain. Occasional noises from behind small leaded windows or within well-fortified quadrangles. Once, like much of Oxford, this had been the fiefdom of a king, Charles I, in the Civil War, as he sought to regroup his failing army in this loyal city. It was a city of martyrs, blood on the streets, and prelates powerful in Church and State, but on that first night, it was for me a shrouded city, satisfyingly draped in a mist which encouraged a sense of romance and genius. The ghostly figures coming out of the mist could have been the returning spirits of those seeking to re-enact their younger days.

In the College dining hall, I had looked up to discover the oak rafters. In the big barn at Sarah's farm there had been such rafters and when we crept in late on some nights we would climb the bales and sink into the ripe silence and life of the newly cut hay. I would look up at those beams as just now in the College. The two scenes intertwined again as I went down a path and looked across the meadows, turned towards the river, the beguiling sound of distant voices, the moon full. Full as it had seemed at Wigton the night Laurie Hill who worked on the dustcart asked me if I could tell him whether the moon was waxing or waning and how I knew. I didn't. He laughed and slapped my back. 'So much for education!' Great Tom, the bell in Christ Church, began its hundred strokes and the sound brought back St Mary's and Wigton and a jolt, a brief kick, of homesickness.

How pathetic. Weeks alone in France working for the Abbé Pierre had brought no such nausea. The Abbé had sent out a call to the young men of Europe to help him in his mission to assist the many *clochards*, tramps, who slept under the bridges of Paris. I went there for a month, the only English volunteer, the others chiefly German. We combed the city for booty and gifts. It was the longest time I had been away from Sarah. Paris had absorbed all the slack with ease.

I walked back to Wadham by way of All Souls and the shroud persisted. Comfortingly. Cyclists, laughter from the pubs, other solitary walkers, a light breeze strengthening. What were the rules about the time you had to get back to the College? We were kept under control from breakfast to bed. I stepped out, the shroud began to dissipate, leaving the last traces of the mist of an autumn night curling across the pavement. Great Tom had finished his heavy chiming, there was a party in one of the rooms in the front quadrangle of the College, lights on. I knew no one.

I was passed by the elderly physics tutor, Dr Keeley. He was on the same staircase as myself. He was one of the few dons remaining who lived in the College as if it were a monastery, the sole survivor of the ancient college-bound days when dons were as penned in as their undergraduates. Rather shaggier than his dog, he was taking the ancient spaniel, Nicholas, for its evening walk past the copper beech tree and into the exclusive Fellows' Garden where Nicholas would do his business while Dr Keeley charged and lit his last pipe of the day and listened, as he said, to the silence.

Chapter Two

I wanted to write how much I missed her, that the occasional 'home' sickness was a sickness for her. But that would have been a whinge. Better to sketch the place out, be as breezy as I felt much of the time, share with her the main mood which flicked to exuberance most of the time in this foreign place and steadily gravitated to contentment. I wanted her to picture the place and eventually, after I had settled in, I wrote.

I wanted Sarah to share it.

The College [I wrote] was founded by Nicholas and Dorothy Wadham, childless West Country religious philanthropists. Before every dinner a long Latin grace is delivered by the Warden joined by a scholar, in praise of them. I'd have to do that one day.

It seems strange to have a 'warden' in charge. Other colleges have presidents or masters or heads or other less grim titles. Our Warden is Sir Maurice Bowra, a beer-barrel-built classics scholar, a writer whose numerous books, one tutor told us in an early meeting, were not always applauded by his contemporaries. This could be envy, the tutor said, the worm in the bud in all universities. Bowra is a man who speaks to everyone as if he were addressing a public meeting, but he's kind-hearted, supportive, cheerfully steamrolling through life.

There are fugitive suggestions of homosexuality. He is a target for rumour and hyperbolic gossip which could be malicious. It spiced his character. It was claimed that when he and the philosopher Isaiah Berlin met to talk, the only way it worked was for their chairs to be back to back. One of the most daring ways to get into the College after hours when the main door was locked was to negotiate a route from the Warden's garden into his house, wait for a quiet opportunity and an open window and bolt through it. One intruder heard Bowra's steps on the staircase and dived behind a sofa. Bowra took down a heavy volume and settled to read, and read on, and on, until he snapped the book shut, stood up and said, 'Switch off the light when you leave, there's a good chap.' And left the room. We relish these Bowraisms.

In the first few weeks he invited new undergraduates to his substantial lodgings in the front quad in groups of about half a dozen. Before he held forth he dealt out sherry, the customary tipple of the university, from a large decanter. Sickly stuff.

When I went to see him, one of our group, an Argentinian called Albert Moth, asked him on what grounds he chose his undergraduates.

Bowra was ready.

'Clever boys,' he said, and beamed as if it included all present. He paused.

'Pretty boys.' He bared his choppers. And then the guillotine finale. The teeth clashed together. 'No shits!' It was spoken to be repeated.

Another World

That settled the matter. We liked that and we liked him more for saying it.

Most of us live in rooms which branch off staircases, all numbered. I'm on Staircase Two. Room Four. Front Quad. There are ten rooms climbing up into the roof. I share my room which I don't like and hadn't bargained for, but that's it. He, Gerald, lives near Oxford and was driven here by his father, a solicitor. He settled in well ahead of the suggested time of arrival. There is a substantial sitting room with two perfect seventeenth-century window seats, one of which overlooks the College gardens, the other monitors the front quadrangle. Two bedrooms, one large, the other a monkish cell. Gerald is another grammar school boy. I suppose the two of us have been lumped together because of that connection. Gerald nabbed the larger and more desirable room, which I think was a bit of a cheat. We ought to have spun for it. He puts on his pyjamas, buttoned up to the neck, at 10 p.m., appears with a hairbrush and makes it clear that a zone of silence should now prevail. He brushes his hair before bed – a perfect parting. When a few of us use the sitting room for a noisy conversation he knocks sharply on his bedroom door. We learn to control our animation or ask him to join us, which takes the heat out of it.

Otherwise he is fine. His face is rather white, tight, strained, the laughter short and dry. In the large shared room there is a three-barred electric fire and some battered furniture. Gerald is *very* fussy. His parents visit him every Saturday, bringing groceries. At first I did not notice how lonely he was. He seems to have no friends and hugs the room. Still, I can work in one of the College or university libraries which are handy and usually under-populated.

One side of the quadrangle is dominated by the dining hall – breakfast, lunch, dinner on the dot, cost included in the scholarship. I've joined the choir but I'm not sure I'll stick it out. It takes too much time. The rugby team is even more demanding – games on Wednesdays and Saturdays, sometimes away; Cambridge, Abingdon's Air Force base, these wipe out most of the day. I like the game and Wadham has a good team and one international but it'll have to go.

Maybe it's ridiculous to say that I am missing Wigton? But I am – I've read that when plants are transplanted they protest. Same as us. And too many men here, most in one age group and somehow cordoned off as if we are recruits being groomed for a regiment and have to learn to parade in step.

And you're not here – for which I'd swap the lot of them. But that's soft. It's an amazing opportunity. At present I'm a bit of an Innocent Abroad. It hasn't settled down to be real yet.

I've come *up* to Oxford. We all do. We will go *up* the ranks and finally, God willing, *up* to Heaven.

Chapter Three

Staircase Two provided my closest friends not only at the university but for years afterwards. There seems no reason for it save the common staircase. Perhaps the fact that all our surnames began with B made for a mysterious connection. Bomford, Bourke, Blaikley and Bragg, all first years and strangers to each other, each strikingly different from the others.

Perhaps our friendship came from constantly bumping into each other as we traipsed up and down the narrow staircase. And it was so easy to go into Hall together for meals and then out for a drink. But something else went on. Our differences seemed to be a strength. Just as, in Wigton, my best friend William was a Tory, a non-reader (later, when he was married, he would say to me, 'Violet [his wife] is the one who reads your books'), unmusical and uninterested in the Deep Platitudes that give teenage life some of its zip. William was a friend who became my closest friend and remained so throughout his life. The same with Eric and my cousin Geoff. Boys whose shoulder you threw your arm around as you walked down the street: always there. No need to investigate it. Something the same began to happen in those first weeks on Staircase Two. Those I met there became the core of my College life.

Robert Bomford was tall, thin, gangly, bespectacled, a zoologist, which meant he had to be in the laboratory at nine. He had been to a relaxed, rather forward-thinking boarding school, Bryanston. He took up rowing for the College and seemed to enjoy the early morning pulling of an oar before breakfast. Robert had a deep considered voice, smoked a pipe and pursued all discussions until they were exhausted, forever saying 'and another point' when we thought that enough had been said. He developed a taste for red wine and became something of a connoisseur. When he sat on a chair, his legs seemed to stretch across the room. It is impossible to think of anyone more good-natured and well-informed. Robert was to do his PhD in Edinburgh. He chose to do his post-doctoral fellowship in Leningrad because he admired the work they did in the Institute of Cytology. Later, under Gorbachev, he changed his scientific interests and went to Tbilisi in Georgia. For three years he organised schools in Russia and made lasting connections.

Robert invited me to stay with him for a few days. His parents were divorced. We went to join his father at his farm in Hampshire. His father had been commissioned in the First World War and been in the thick of it. In manner he was a characteristic county gentleman but his expertise made him an outstandingly progressive farmer. Robert told me proudly that he owned the first combine harvester in Hampshire and took on the tough chalk land which he had inherited with a zest that transformed it into a very modern concern.

He was a collector of clocks and it was there that I learned about the Wigton clocks which had studded the town and district in Cumberland unnoticed. But here they were memorialised in a fat volume of the best of British clocks.

Wigton was famous! Wall clocks but more especially long case, or grandfather, clocks emblazoned with names from the town. I was embarrassed and proud when Mr Bomford produced, in one of his books of nineteenth-century British clocks, the pages on the largely unknown (to me) local Wigton clockmakers. Our grandfather clocks had made it into the superior world of a distinguished clock collection along with the gentlemanly furniture in Robert's house! The hard ticking, the tocking and then the chimes were a gentle orchestra. When I made enough money, much later on, I sought out and eventually bought a longcase Wigton clock. It still ticks and tocks; it still chimes.

On the way back from his father's we called in to see his mother Madeleine in Hampstead. She let out rooms in her large house and wrote for the newspapers about opera and the latest plays. She was very generous in taking me along with Robert to the Royal Opera House. It was to be the first of several visits to opera. Before this, I had only heard opera on records a local man brought to the Anglican Young People's Association (AYPA) now and then.

At the Royal Opera House I thought I was going into a palace. Many of the men wore evening dress. Madeleine gently suggested I wear my suit. The women were dressed to impress. The place itself glowed a palatial splendour, but most of all, after the first notes were struck, there was a performance which spun my head around. It was *La traviata*.

I had been wary of 'classical' music even though in the church choir in Wigton I had sung anthems every week. But church was different. Singing opera had always sounded unnatural. Why strain your voice so much? What was wrong with a natural voice? I thought opera singers tried too hard and were affected. In a school debate I'd argued that, if trained, Elvis could be Mario Lanza, but however well trained, Mario Lanza could never be Elvis, because Elvis's talent was given, not engineered. And wasn't opera reserved for the Few? But *La traviata* was so different. I had been led into a hitherto alien world made real, made moving, immersing.

Opera voices, of which I'd heard snatches on the Third Programme, where the effort of making the sounds seemed to get in the way of the sense, all naturalness suppressed, had turned me off – but not here, not that night with Robert and his mother. All that was gone moments after the monumental curtains parted and the opera began. It was something so different, based on what was so fundamentally the same. I was wrung dry. Opera was to wonder at from then on. Even now I thank Robert's mother, and when the final applause petered out, all I wanted was to see it again.

She also took us occasionally to West End plays. She knew that world well and I was introduced to it with a flourish. She would also throw away remarks about other critics at the opera: one, for instance, who would 'always take his pyjamas with him'. What did that mean? She was of a class alongside Mrs Cavaghan, a woman my mother had cleaned for. Mrs Cavaghan lived in a grand Georgian house near Wigton. Her husband had been killed just after the outbreak of the war. She was the most glamorous person I had ever met. Robert's mother, Madeleine, was her London twin. Looking back now, I can see she liked to educate Robert and myself through metropolitan glamour and often mischievous gossip, always wanting to deliver a minor shock. I think she played us like fish. Perhaps that was where Robert's passion for fly-fishing came from! I liked her very much. She was so lively and open.

It was while at Madeleine's house that I saw an edition of the BBC arts programme *Monitor*. I had never seen the programme before. It featured Robert Graves and had been shot on Majorca. It had an instant and lasting effect. Somehow I thought that all great poets were dead, but here was Robert Graves writing in the sun, stripped to the waist, a straw hat giving him, I thought, the True Poetic look. And, most of all, we saw his pen scrolling out the poem 'Flying Crooked' – just like that! An empty page, then a poem! Sun. A straw hat. A poem. And that, I thought, is how it's done!

I invited Robert Bomford to come to Wigton for a few days. My mother made up my single bed for two – a pillow at each end – as was usual when my cousin Geoff came.

When I saw the bed in that cell of my room so neatly reordered, I had a hunch, a certainty, even a dread that this would not do. The bedroom next door to mine had been Andrew's and was now vacant. Andrew, who had lodged with us, had left. His repeated petty thefts had finally overruled my mother's clamp of loyalty and my father had had enough. Andrew had been part of my life from the start. He and my mother – both illegitimate – had been fostered by Mrs Gilbertson and Andrew took on the role of my mother's 'brother'. He was sallow, rough-tongued, lonely and condemned to do the dirtiest shift work at the factory. He made me lavish promises he very rarely kept. He lied a lot. I was distraught when my father showed him the door. My mother's objections were, uniquely, ignored.

I can remember clearly the struggle it took to find the words to describe my resistance to the two-in-a-single-bed for Robert and myself. Eventually I suggested to my mother that perhaps it would be better if Robert had Andrew's empty room. That was all. That was it. She seemed a little surprised but popped him in the back room. I experienced the loosening of a very tight knot of obscure anxiety . . .

Robert was keen to get into the Lake District. He had brought his fishing rod and a tin of bait. It was a pursuit in which I had no interest. Robert was passionate about it and the Lakes were too famous to miss. But he slept in for the vital early bus.

I went across the road to the bus stop with my mother, who asked the driver if he could wait for a minute or two. Time passed. To my mother the conductor said, 'Sorry, Ethel, but we have to set off.' Just as the bus began to move, out came Robert, shirt unbuttoned, shoelaces undone, face full of consternation, long fishing rod somehow carried alongside the packet of sandwiches my mother had prepared for him. He began to pursue the bus up King Street. His long galumping strides would have made little headway but the conductor took pity and stopped the double-decker halfway up the street, opposite the Vaults. Robert made it, with a cascade of apologies.

My mother never forgot the scene. She liked Robert and this image sealed him into her memory forever.

Later, when she told the story, she would always add, 'He was very good mannered, was Robert.'

* * *

Ulick Bourke, Irish descent, former Head Boy at Wellington College, walked – all but marched – upright, brisk, alert, like the soldier he had been intended for. The best word I can find to describe him is 'true'. Like his father and those before him, it was assumed that he would join the army, quickly earn a commission and rise to a high rank. He had corn-coloured hair, short back and sides, a smile that was inward, as if it hid an unquenchable and secret spring of contentment. He played hockey. He didn't rate the College's teaching as highly as that he had experienced at school. He had friends from school at other colleges but seemed quite content with Staircase Two. It was easy to make him laugh.

At that time Britain could still claim to be at the top table. Churchill was credited with having steered it there. After two wars and a bitter interval of turbulence and poverty, it seemed to be re-emerging even post-Suez as a force to be respected, despite the jibe that it had 'lost an empire but not found a role'. It was confident in its own skin.

The worldwide Empire was still a factor. Those in charge were at best in a mould of imperial public service, while those who had made up the millions of armed forces and the industrial mass had voted through a radical new socialist state starring the Health Service. Though battered, unbowed, though brutally bombed and blitzed, still claiming a victory, the country seemed ready to resume something of its soul and destined role. People such as Ulick were being trained to serve and secure it.

A couple of years into our three-year course he brought Eileen, his girlfriend, to Wadham, where his friends immediately took to her fine English rose looks, her dry comments, her independence, her gift of undercutting us all in an argument. She was, as his friends had anticipated, a 'corker'. Widely read, an autodidact, good company. Ulick, we agreed, was a lucky man.

They married soon after he graduated and he went out of my life until near the very end of his. His death shook us all. It seems to me that he conducted his passage through appalling difficulties with such grace. There was about him an extreme example of an honourable stoicism which I do not think I have come across before or since. I asked Eileen to write a few words about Ulick's last years.

> After Oxford Ulick taught history for three years in Rome which left him with a lifelong love of Italy. He then changed career and qualified as a lawyer and thereafter lived in Brussels for twenty-five years, during which time he specialised in international trade law. Not only did this job take him all over the world, thus satisfying his desire to travel, but it also gave him enormous satisfaction both intellectually and personally. He relished establishing an office which was truly international and, on a personal level, making enduring friendships as a result.
>
> Unfortunately, Ulick's career as a lawyer came to an abrupt halt in his mid-fifties when he had a brain haemorrhage. Following multiple surgeries, he rallied as best he could for a number of years. However, a second blow was in store when motor neurone symptoms appeared and the slow and inexorable decline to death began.
>
> I told Melvyn that in Ulick's last days I asked him if he'd like to see a priest. I suppose it was our far-off

Anglican upbringing that prompted me to do this. Ulick simply smiled at me and made a shooing away gesture with his hand (because of course he had no speech by then). I'm sure it was meant to indicate to me that if it turned out that there *was* anything beyond this life, then he would deal with it unaided. He didn't want priestly advice or prayers; he'd just cope with it if it happened, as he had coped with his illnesses.

He became his own battlefield and just as his father had been prepared to fight to the last man in two great battles of World War II – one in the North African desert and the other in Kohima – so could you see Ulick fighting to the last. His struggle was and remains so clear in my memory. I went to see him in those last months. He was an inspiration. I can still 'see' Ulick on his small tractor roaring through the field around his house in the Cotswolds in his last months after he had taken early retirement. I can see him now, being driven by his illness from side to side on our walks in a narrow country lane near his house. He was remorselessly brought down, never giving in. Always the smile, sometimes grim, but never lost. No complaints. None. I miss him still.

* * *

Alan Blaikley was the most mysterious of the four of us. Plump, given to no exercise whatsoever, thoughtful in his throwaway, unaffected, rather clerical, Victorian way, son of an American mother and an English father who had fought in the Artists Rifles in the First World War and landed up in Hampstead Garden Suburb, North London, an idealistic housing scheme. Alan was educated at local private boys' schools. He had a knack for turning Greek and Latin verses into colloquial, catchy English, which served him well when he left Oxford after only one year for failing the trip-wire exams of the second term, designed to weed out the bluffers and the slackers. Alan was neither. Oxford bored him. He wanted out. The best way was to construct an effective exit. Examination failure was his solution.

He went back to what he and his best friend Ken Howard had begun at their prep school. They became professional partners, writing pop songs. In his solemn almost donnish way Alan preached to the world on the quality of pop songs: their deceptive simplicity, their clever elision of sound and sense, the voice of the working class, he said, 'at last', the new culture they were creating and above all their slyly concealed sexual rudeness, which he liked to dig out. 'Mostly,' he would say in that churchy voice, 'they are to do with copulation. This is often cleverly disguised. The only serious objection I have is to the use of the word "baby". I find it distressing.' Over the years Ken and Alan wrote songs for Elvis Presley, but mostly for a group they assembled for their own work – 'Have I The Right?' was their biggest hit. Elsewhere they wrote 'Bend It!', used by Gilbert and George for a performance piece. They wrote for television serials and for a musical which blazed into the West End with *Mardi Gras* but wilted in an unairconditioned theatre in the 1970s scorcher summer. They were prolific and original. Alan wrote an autobiography largely consisting of footnotes.

The Warden, Maurice Bowra, tried to persuade Alan to

take a break and return in the autumn to redo his Prelims – that low hurdle of exams in the second term. He would certainly pass. Alan reported that Bowra said in their tête-à-tête in his lodgings that this was merely a temporary lapse, not uncommon. He then gave Alan a copy of his latest book, on Greek tragedy, inscribed 'We look forward to welcoming you back soon'.

When recounting this the next day, Alan said how tempted he had been to say yes. But he went on, 'Oxford is not for me.' He had talked it over with his father, who encouraged him to 'go his own way'.

We were sitting on a bench under the monumental copper beech tree in one of the Wadham gardens. Alan had asked me there to talk about his decision. What did I think?

He was very nervous, looking away, somehow simultaneously distracted and concentrated.

Out of the blue, he said very forcefully, 'I can't stand this place a day longer! It's snobbish, hypocritical and dull!'

I didn't want to contradict him. His mind was closed.

He looked at me carefully.

After a deep breath, with emphatic steadiness, he looked around and then said, 'I am homosexual.'

At that time homosexuality was a crime punished by the law and leading to imprisonment. There had recently been a notorious case in Oxford where it was not uncommonly illegally practised. Alan's confession was a risk.

I felt winded. I remember that I did not know at first what to say. After a few moments, I held out my hand and we shook, as if concluding a treaty. It was not until some days later that I understood what an effort it had been for him and what an honour for me.

I am sure that I stuttered something like 'that's all right' or – even worse! – 'I don't mind.' Whatever. We had shaken hands and that said everything.

'I rather fancy a drink,' he said. I nodded. Perfect. 'Not here,' Alan said, indicating the College, 'not in that cellar bar with the rugger buggers or in any of the usual haunts. There's a place down near the Green that I like. You've probably never heard of it.'

We walked purposefully through the centre of the city as if to an urgent meeting. I had never been to this pub. It was late lunchtime midweek but still noticeably busy. Scotch eggs and lager and appreciative nods to Alan. It was unusually polite. We too had a lager and a scotch egg, and found a corner.

'It's raided now and then,' said Alan, not without a little pride, 'but they never find enough proof.'

He was relaxed, as if he had cast off body armour.

'You must come and meet my father,' he said. 'I told him some of the stories you told me about your grandfather in the First World War. He's drawing a panel of faces from the trenches. It would be very helpful if you could bring along a photo or two.'

'I think I might be able to dig one out.'

'Another?'

Alan, who usually sipped rather than gulped, had shifted the lager already.

'I'll wait.'

'I'll bring a half for you anyway.'

He stood up and looked around proprietorially, happy.

Another World

'Thank you.' He nodded his head. 'I knew you'd be . . .' He hesitated. 'Better than understanding. Just feel good about it.' He glanced over the clientele and his happiness went up the scale. 'I like it here,' he said, wholly casting off the cassock of respectability. 'There's risk, I like that too. And' – his smile broadened – '*and sex*.' He laughed out loud. So, I hope, did I.

Chapter Four

The window seats in our room, set in the wall, represented class, leisure, breeding and wealth. Prop a cushion behind you, stretch your legs over a thin mattress and look through the small leaded panes of glass into the front quadrangle of the College, dominated by a 'do not use' lawn and by the sets of rooms which housed the young gentlemen, and you could scan your new world. It was a voyeur's nest, or rather like a sniper's hidden perch, all the more enjoyable for being unseen while seeing everything in the marketplace of the quad – the scholars and commoners, gowned, most of them, ambling but sure of their direction, a shuffle and reshuffling of bodies, like watching the same scene rearrange itself ceaselessly. It could be mesmeric.

I had the room to myself on most mornings as Gerald scooted off to queue for a good desk at the Radcliffe Camera, the most popular university library; its span and its large domed ceiling housed many thousands of books that could not be borrowed but had to be read inside the library. In the early days I used to queue along with Gerald but the worker beehive experience inside the library was too distracting. Better if I could secure the weekly reading list and find a nook and a desk of my own in a lesser library, preferably inside the College.

For historians there were three tutorials a fortnight from the key tutor. For each one we were given a list of a number of books and articles thought necessary by the tutor for that one-to-one encounter with the don. Once a week we ploughed through the history of the British Isles in a course called 'Modern History 412 AD to 1832' – from the year the Romans left to the year Parliament dipped its toe into democracy. The evidence along the way was voluminous, the critical commentaries just as bulky.

After each one-hour weekly session the tutor would provide another list of a few books and several articles we could refer to or not for the following week's essay. These essays would be read aloud, tête-à-tête, and take at most half an hour. The tutor would then dissect your essay, challenge it, repair it. You could argue that with a world to study, this close inspection of such a small part of it was disproportionate. But it was claimed that it taught you to handle evidence and how to test it.

Once a fortnight we would be required to give a similar treatment to European history, 1485 onwards, or philosophy – Aristotle and Machiavelli, for example. That too demanded intense reading if you were not to fall flat on your face. These tutorials could take place with the experts in their field from other colleges. None of it was a cakewalk. You were marked in Greek letters – beginning alpha, beta, gamma, delta, sometimes alpha-beta or beta-alpha. To talk one to one with such distinguished scholars was a privileged system and if you wanted to keep up you had to put in the hours. There was nowhere to hide.

At the end of the second term there were exams – Prelims – to weed out those who had crept into the university under the wire in the entrance exams and interviews: Alan was one of the very few people who failed them – deliberately. After that we were exam-free until Finals at the end of the third year.

At school, Mr James's method of teaching history was to deliver a short lecture to the class, invariably dividing the subject into three sections (there were three reasons for every event in Mr James's universe: the beginning, the continuation and the conclusion). An inevitable historical trinity. I've kept the habit. After that he would ask for or provoke questions. The senior tutor I had at Wadham was Lawrence Stone. His method was the opposite. We undergraduates would park ourselves in a comfortable chair in his rich theatrical room and read our essays aloud. It was based on our weekly reading of the books and articles listed the previous week. It could be awkward when you realised how crass you had been or plain embarrassing when you caught yourself out in clumsy formulations, spotted them a line or two in advance and tried to swerve around them or substitute a better phrase on the spot. But it had its advantages.

Perhaps this came from Kipling. His advice was that what you wrote ought to be read aloud, if only to yourself, before you let anyone else hear it. More likely, I guess, like much else in the Oxford system, it could be traced back to the versicle and responses in mediaeval prayer. While you read there were no interruptions.

Then, Mr Stone would begin a discussion by dismantling what you had assembled. I remember him being patient, careful and providing the best phase of the tutorial. Occasionally I scribbled a few words as an aide-memoire for future reading; mostly I concentrated on trying to keep up.

It was hopeless in any equal sense but somehow the tutor let you in and you could have your say. Mr Stone – like many of the tutors at that time – had spent active time in the war and now and then laced his remarks on our past rulers with 'they were just a bunch of shits'. Shits were common to ex-servicemen and somehow seemed purged of any common or odorous association.

By the end of the tutorial – if you had been lucky – there was a sense of comradeship and scholarship, however slight, which was just the little flattery that you wanted, and you could seem to be equals. That was the best of it, an unspoken deal, and whenever you felt that you had, in some way, done just that, the bounce of satisfaction was the wage. For those moments we could imagine or persuade ourselves we were on the way to becoming scholars.

I never took to the big libraries. Working on my own was the best method, sealed in myself, undisturbed. The window seat was a place in which I could work hard. The room was silent, empty, mine. Several thoughts or what passed for thought could filter through without the obstacle and disturbance of other people.

It was also perfect for drifting, for sifting through the days in this unique and separate place. I was becoming used to seeing so many undergraduates in the streets, most in their black gowns. Beneath that university uniform was a second near-enough uniform of sports jacket and cavalry twill trousers, brogues and school or College ties as part of the ensemble. They could seem like a specialised sect, and yet soon I dressed near enough as they did. I was being assimilated. I nodded to no one, just as no one nodded back, unlike a 'walk up street' in Wigton where a variety of recognitions were registered repeatedly. There were occasional groups and conversation but mostly these formed a self-absorbed cluster, deliberately distant as if determined not to be infected by others. Or that might have been just the way I interpreted what I saw. Yet it seemed the reality. It was not unfriendly. Just keeping themselves to themselves on intrusive streets. It was almost as if they were a species apart and had to behave as apart. Or had been drilled into apartness at their schools, or saw apartness as a safety-first method. There was little room for a casual encounter.

Was there snobbery in the air? Of course. England is cemented on fine degrees of snobbery. I found it the High Snobbery of the traditional ruling generation, neither bruising nor even mildly offensive. It was easy to ignore. I thought it was the predictable pose of superiority for those who had no class. We were soon aware of sons and daughters of the titled, landed and the very rich, some of whom treated the colleges and were treated by the colleges as members of a finishing school. Naturally the close packing of boarding-school life, in some cases from seven to seventeen, had been a key factor in moulding their character. Just as the grammar school in Wigton had influenced mine. The differences really took wing after university, when the old tribalisms kicked in and centuries of segregation provided well-worn tracks of advancement for some and the influence of Oxford was not all-powerful. Inheritance trumped scholarship. Their worlds had been sorted out long before university.

The intricate ins and outs of privilege, of real and assumed superiority, went on but it was up to you to decide whether or not you wanted to follow the scent. Many groups were ships that passed in the night. Such snobbery could be understood as the mere clannishness of old friends and familiars from boyhood and accepted as yet another Old Pals gang among the many up and down the social scale. It could be the old tribal matter, Britain reverting to its Norman Conquest state. It could be a clique, a cordoned-off group dug into its own sufficient and satisfied view of itself.

It could be ignored and it was, in my experience, by many of us. It was as if we had grown out of it. People were content to make their own way with those they discovered as part of their own crowd or fitted in to others without friction. And Oxford encouraged new perspectives as well as old. It could be rigid in one instance and elastic in another. Which is next to saying that it did not matter unless you made it matter. Not to ignore the undoubted presence of snobs who considered themselves 'a cut above'. Some of them would be happily stuck with that delusion for a lifetime.

* * *

David shared a set of rooms on the ground floor of Staircase Two. He was imposingly tall, handsome, always an inward man. On one Saturday night I had been leaving to join Robert, Ulick and Alan in the King's Arms or the Eagle and Child. It was a sunny evening. David was leaning against the doorway, the sun on his face. We talked and then I asked him to come along and join us. He shrugged away the suggestion. I persisted. So did he. I told him what a great place the Bird and Baby was, the nickname for the Eagle and Child, renowned as the pub that hosted a group of dons skilled in Old English who produced *The Hobbit* and *The Lion, the Witch and the Wardrobe* and much else as they sank beer in the back bar. No go. Finally realising that

I was outstaying my welcome, I left. His refusal had been lowkey but implacable, underlined by his easy elegance as he leaned against the doorway. He could have made me feel a fool but didn't. That happened afterwards when I recollected what an ignorant pest I had been.

It was not a big college and the gossip was gentle. A little biting but harmless. Soon after that evening, possibly in a drowse on the window seat, it clicked and I realised it had been the Sabbath and that David was Jewish. Not to know that at eighteen . . . and at Wadham! Why such ignorance, after being raised listening to readings from the Old Testament every morning at school assembly, twice a day on Sundays, and singing the psalms of David. Beginning history with Adam and Eve! And I had had no idea of the history behind David's refusal or the general knowledge about the Sabbath!

Wadham housed several Jewish scholars and cultural activists. Mike Kustow, for example, who was a walking, talking, bubbling-over encyclopaedia of contemporary culture, later to sweep into the lists of the new experimental television channel, Channel 4. It was run for some time by another Jewish cultural guru, Jeremy Isaacs. In Wadham itself there was Alan Coren, a generous, amiable man and an effortlessly brilliant scholar who picked up a scholarship to Harvard and returned to edit *Punch* in its prime; Michael Elstein, who won a place at the famous Polish Academy of Film-Making; and Michael Wolfers . . .

In Wigton there had been only one Jewish boy at my school. Perhaps to make his mark, he bought a motorbike as soon as he could and drove roaringly around Wigton on a Sunday, a town at that time immured in its own obedient religious silences in a dozen places of worship. The choice of that empty afternoon was a challenge. After two or three Sundays he stopped. I presumed that there had been protests. He had ripped the Sunday silence apart.

As a dedicated Christian, I was doused in Judaism. At Sunday School and school, passages from the Old Testament and New were read aloud and the names – widely adopted in Wigton – Isaac, Joseph and Mary, David, my hero throughout school life, the Apostles, all of them save Judas – and then Esther and Eve. There was a Solomon in the town, an Adam, a Jacob, Jesse . . . Alongside the names was the profound, magnificent and infinitely complex story of two thousand years based on centuries of pre-Christian culture, succeeded by a New Testament which was seeded in a small town, not unlike Wigton. Our twelve places of worship in the town were all led by Jesus, by a total belief in the birth, crucifixion and resurrection of Jesus Christ. We very rarely referred to him as a Jew. The root of a faith which from that all but invisible starting seed inside the Roman Empire grew to glories and disasters, to violence and cruelty and to a visionary future, arts, scholarship, philosophy, a miracle of survival – what did Jewish scholars *not* affect, even define? And there we were too.

By the time I reached Wadham I had had what could have been called a Sound Education, including familiarity with the Old Testament. Yet I had failed to understand why David was so resolute on that Saturday night.

* * *

I have written admiringly of the history teacher Mr James, whose energy and dedication changed the lives of many pupils.

Shelley rather boasted that 'Poets are the unacknowledged legislators of the world'. Only up to a point in my opinion. Teachers far more effectively fulfil that role, and I will back up the claim.

I have interviewed hundreds of artists, writers, musicians and painters, and in innumerable cases they have emphasised the following four words – 'there was this teacher'. This teacher who lit the flame of encouragement, who spotted where support was needed, who pointed out the path that could be taken. The crown of unacknowledged legislators, in my experience, goes to the teachers who have shaped minds. There are many – I have mentioned Mr James – and, as so often, they are founded on the unfathomable genii of Greece: Socrates, Plato, Aristotle – only the headliners of a cluster of men in a small town at a particular time, speaking an accessible language, who changed thought, empowered logical curiosity in all matters, the idea of thought and its reach.

And its reach stretched out to our school, above all through Mr James.

He put university within our grasp – not just Oxford and Cambridge, but Durham, Manchester, Leeds. Those he inspired entered the lists throughout the UK.

* * *

Two of the more unexpected protégés of Mr James were Bill Jefferson and Pauline Prince.

Bill because he won his place on a modern languages ticket although that did not prevent him from expressing his gratitude to Mr James, as did Pauline Prince who came from a difficult background and became one of the first women to gain a place at Wadham.

Bill was a one-off. He came from the village of Abbeytown, built around a mostly ruined abbey; the abbey church was still functional – Bill played the organ there. He also played the piano and the guitar, with which he serenaded his girlfriend outside her house now and then. He was a fine-looking man, gracious, a scholar, rather amused by those of us who rushed and pushed our way. He liked gambling and once challenged the College Bursar to spin, double or quits, over a term's fee.

He went into the British Council, retired to Silloth, four miles from his birthplace, where he lived in a fine terraced house overlooking the green and beyond to the sea. There was an ease, even something of a swagger, about him from his walk to his talk, which was attractive and enviable.

Pauline was Mr James's pride and joy. She was brought up in Water Street in Wigton, the heart of the web of old, crowded, damp, intensely cramped and inadequate housing in the middle of the town. Her father had a flat cart and a pony and traded in goods from local farms. Her mother was a friend of my mother's. She was never well; her illness was unremitting and it became clear in Pauline's last couple of years in school that her mother was terminally ill. It must have been a remorseless struggle for Pauline to get to Wadham and she never ceased to thank Mr James. She organised Wigton–Wadham reunions; she found ways to make sure his quality was recognised. She was the most exceptional of all his pupils and outstandingly pretty. She went on to teach. We kept in touch. Our proud mothers liked to exchange gossip about us.

Chapter Five

The most singular person I met at Oxford was Michael Wolfers.

He always wore a suit and tie. He played no sports. His renown in the university was based on phenomenal attendance at parties which he wrote up in memorable terms for university newspapers. His smile was vivid and wide, a gash of warmth, generous, almost beseeching. Both his parents – who were Jewish – had been killed in Germany just before the outbreak of World War II. English connections provided him with guardians and a place at a Quaker boarding school. He was a remarkable mixture of the most gregarious and the most isolated man I met. His subject was law.

We met in unusual circumstances. The College locked down at 10.30 p.m. I had come back from a debate at the Oxford Union. My first. The Union was its own parliament constructed as a formal debating chamber and seeded over the years by undergraduates who would sometimes bloom into notable politicians not only in Great Britain but across the old Empire. It played its part in the imperial superstructure.

My experience at the Union had been intimidating. I had imagined that you stood up and said your bit and cheered those whose side you were on. Instead, I met a white-tied, formally dressed platoon of young men my age who spoke like weathered orators and gave the proceedings not only the air but the character of practised politicians way above their age and out of my reach. They were on another plane. The idea of making a contribution melted away in the first half hour. I endured the full debate, schooling myself to patience while the grandeur rolled on and my resolution grew that I never could and never would be able to join in such a performance.

I'd heard that if you stayed on to the end then just anyone could jump up and have their brief say, but the well-rehearsed and ritualistic pace of the opening speeches and impressively confident formalities floored me for good. I never went again. That night I dawdled back to the College. It was still the first term and in the misty evenings I liked best, Oxford appeared to rise out of the earth like Excalibur.

The College gate was locked. I knew that the traditional way in was to go round to the back, heave over a wall, navigate through the buildings in the new quad, and head for one of the two alleys to the old. We had been told that this was flouting the College laws and subject to a fine. Few bothered about that. For some reason, after pacing back and forth in front of the main gate I hung around – perhaps I thought someone would come out and I could pop in as they popped out. It would be easier and legal.

As I passed by a ground-floor window for the third time, it was lifted open and a voice said, 'You can get in this way if you'd like.'

I straddled the sill and all but fell into a room heaving with books.

'I was just making myself some coffee. Would you like a cup?'

He switched on a bar of the electric fire which took a fraction of the chill off the room. A second bar helped make it rather less spartan.

'I'm Michael,' he said, and giggled. 'I know your name. There are biscuits.'

He had an intense affectionate manner which I found impossible not to like, although the warmth of it and the self-interruptions of a giggle could raise eyebrows. In that context, Michael's navy blue suit seemed a radical statement. Soon I was to guess that the giggle was the nervous consequence of a miserably assailed childhood which emerged in fractions of our conversation. I was to understand he had been too deeply hurt too young and even now flinched at the memories.

I took to him from the start. We engaged in that cliché of student life – the 'talking through the night'. He was outstandingly clever.

Michael asked questions and had the knack of taking my answers into his own answers as if to put me at my ease. He sensed I was open to being educated in the ways of the university and appointed himself my life tutor. Immediately he asked me how I was settling down among so many public schoolboys.

All I knew about the behaviour of public schoolboys had been found in books, in *Jennings and Darbishire*, *The Fifth Form at St Dominic's*, *Tom Brown's School Days* and especially *Mike* by P.G. Wodehouse. These schools were on the whole friendly, fear-free, upright places, secure in sound values, confirmed in sport, especially cricket, and full of robust good fun – a coherent corps. The occasional bullies were the exception and always put in their place. Flashman figured as the prime example of a bad egg.

Oxford, behind the traditional façade, was like a jazz band with several soloists only now and then joining together in harmony: on the whole what you could do mattered as much as where you came from, though this generalisation was gathered from a distance. Close up, if and when questioning occurred, it could be condescending, patronising, spiky or just nervous. Nothing to worry about.

Michael's great talent was to cultivate friendship. I left his room in the lightening early hours, engrossed in the capacious company he had provided, already linked by his gift for instant and intense friendship.

We kept track of each other. He was to win a 'promising young journalist' award which took him to the north of England, to a year's employment on a northern newspaper. It might be said that he 'fell' for the north and for the working class – whom, like George Orwell, he got to know by working among them. He recognised the best of their qualities which his fine manners appreciated. 'You ought to write about them,' he said. 'They are underrepresented in our middle-class literature.' He won another award and came back to London where he was soon writing for a major newspaper. I saw him regularly at that time.

Then he disappeared. Just like that. No farewell, no discussion, no forwarding address nor information for about two months.

His story was that the British Council had offered him yet another scholarship to work in West Africa. He took to it as enthusiastically as he had taken to the north of England. In his letters he described the people as warm, inclusive, effortlessly democratic.

He mastered two of the local African languages within a few months, more would follow. He moved around the continent. Significantly, when I look back, he was always where the British interest was involved and needed local information. When he returned to London 'on leave' we met and he was brimful of the goodness of the people he had met, their gentleness and their brilliance. In one posting he had bought a set of football jerseys for a local boys' team which made him Honorary President. He became an attentive football supporter – this a man who had never kicked a football in his life. After two years, with a bequest from his foster-father, he bought a small house in London in that riddle of working-class terraces behind Waterloo Station. That was his lock-up den for the rest of his life.

More visits to Africa. Back home, heavy involvement in the local Labour Party in Waterloo, its meetings and its marches. Friends from Oxford were invited to his den and we went happily for a frugal encounter. He drank very little and seemed to think everyone should do the same: or more likely he couldn't afford it. There was no outward appearance of material comfort. You went to see and talk to Michael because you liked him, enjoyed his conversation and felt better, braced, after you had seen him. His social circle was wide and not undistinguished.

We used to go out to lunch at a cheap restaurant. It could drag out until teatime.

He also saw Alan regularly. Now and then Alan and I would try to figure out what he was actually doing in his sweeps across North and West Africa.

Years on, I asked a dozen of my friends in London to a birthday dinner at the Garrick Club. Michael flew back from Africa to be there. He arrived very early and was unusually eager to catch up. I thought there was what might be described as a 'disturbance' about him. He had always been a little portly but now the fat seemed to be gaining control. He wanted to hold on to our conversation, almost clinging to it, but others turned up and we went to the round table in the private room – silver-candled, the walls supporting a dense display of London scenes over the last two centuries.

Did I notice that he had one or two glasses of champagne? He was no drinker. Or that he was sweating heavily? Or that his speech, always fast and clever, speeded up? Some did.

Suddenly he collapsed face down on the table.

The ambulance arrived. We witnessed the speed of three big men reviving him and kneading him back to life. A stretcher lifted and carried him through a near-silent Garrick Club out onto the street, into the ambulance and away. I watched it drive away, siren wailing. Then I found an empty room. I burst into tears . . .

I tried, and others tried, to track down where he had gone. It should have been easy. But the Charing Cross Hospital had no comment. Nor had any other.

The event got into the *Daily Mail*.

Someone made a bob or two: it was an accurate description of the event. I was sure of the perpetrator but let it lie. I hated it but on the positive side I thought it might bring out some helpful information. None came.

The funeral was at the crematorium at Golders Green. It was impressively well attended. Afterwards we went to a wake in the Freemasons Arms in Hampstead. What surprised me then and still does is that the majority of the people were strangers to each other. There was a strong feeling of an intellectual Jewish presence of a high order. There were others whom I had never seen but heard of, and, after the introductions at the wake, I never met again. Michael's life was skilfully compartmentalised.

What happened next was something we – Alan and myself – had often joked about. Word came that he had been a spy. Soon after the funeral there was a spread in a South African newspaper writing about the 'death of an English spy'.

Alan and I tried to verify it without success.

It made sense.

Someone claiming to be a 'cousin' of Michael's came to see me a couple of months afterwards to ask about Michael. He confessed that – in his view – there was no question but that Michael had been a spy. He wanted me to help him piece together a biography. I refused.

Two letters from his old school friends in the month or so after the event. After that, silence and a continuing sense of loss.

Michael and his uncompleted story.

That window into his room at Wadham, forever hard to pass by.

* * *

There were others I got to know in that first term – always in the College, as if it were a walled village. A few of these would continue as lifelong friends. Peter Copping for instance, who read history, as I did, but whose range seemed unlimited. Not only history but physics, politics old and new, economics, astronomy . . . Someone said he had a mind like a jukebox. You popped in your questions, it whirred around and out came an answer. His father was a gardener in Kent. At four, Peter had suffered a severe attack of meningitis which had left him permanently very hard of hearing, bordering on deaf. It was a terrible affliction. As a consequence, he shouted loudly in normal conversation, hoping, I guess, that we would shout back so that we could be understood. It could have cut him off from lectures, plays, music, the general babble of talk in the Junior Common Room. But he joined in. He would not be denied. At times he must have felt desperate.

A few years later, when Lisa and I were married, he would come to our house in Kew Gardens on a Saturday or Sunday evening and find, I hoped, a sort of peace. The marvel was that he let his affliction stop him at nothing from the time I met him at Oxford. Screwing in his latest hearing aid he would walk off to the theatre or cinema and sit at the front of the stalls; concerts did not daunt him and even microphone-free lectures in vast halls were lassoed into his life. After he graduated he found a post at Manchester Metropolitan University where he also managed to put together a life that gave him fuller satisfaction. I worked in Manchester for a while and saw him at his most determined not to be denied a full, normal life. A well-liked and conscientious tutor, eccentric but fearless in the racy adventures the young Manchester offered. He became a Friend of the Hallé Orchestra and attended many concerts, again on the front row. As his condition deteriorated he must have felt increasing pressure. Towards the end, he could not hold on. The strain of insisting on

Another World

normality was – and increasingly vividly showed that it was – too much, too much. He wore himself down.

* * *

From the window seat I saw them come and go. Some of them brilliant men – John Caute, for instance, who in one summer – while still an undergraduate – published a widely appreciated political novel drawn from his military service pre-Oxford in West Africa, got a First Class degree in history in a period when only about ten First Class degrees were awarded in a squad of more than three hundred history undergraduates, and was elected to the pyramidical pinnacle of All Souls College. I would see him strolling across the quad, idly swishing a squash racquet. Or Julian Mitchell, another history First, who while still at university published stories with Faber & Faber, before graduating to reel off television classics. He would stop and chat to everyone he met.

And of course there were the dons, the tutors, the fellows.

They, gowned and unhurried, brought a particular style to the place. Maybe they walked more thoughtfully, certainly rather more slowly. Of course they were older, possibly ever increasingly weary of the repetitive compulsions of their teaching load.

My principal tutor, Lawrence Stone, could have been portrayed by El Greco. The lean, intelligent face, something explosive inside him covered up by a gentle exterior and patience. Or he could have been hooded and in monk's habit. God alone knows how he had the patience to listen to our essays, by the dozen, every week.

Like other tutors, he talked to undergraduates one-to-one for an hour, above twenty times a week. There were eight of us reading history in each of the three years, about two dozen all told. Looking back, I can't fathom where he found the stamina to endure these adolescent offerings. He was building what would turn out to be an outstanding career with original interpretations of seventeenth-century English history and the role of women in that history. He entered with vigour the lists of the current Oxford running battle about the Rise of the Gentry. How he blocked out boredom at our offerings beggars the imagination.

We were spoiled. Mr Stone's room was above the entrance to the College. You wound up a tight spiralling stone staircase and there waiting before you was the room reported to have been used by Christopher Wren and other scholars and inventors who had initiated the Royal Society there three hundred years previously. We entered a shrine. Wadham had been a key location in the establishment of the Royal Society and the Society a key factor in the development and communication of the sciences.

So how did we begin?

Mr Stone was always good tempered. I don't know how he managed that either. Perhaps it was experience in the war. At school I had been taught by ex-servicemen, at home and in the pub the collective was ex-service, and here at Oxford the pattern continued. I think it bred a willingness to support the younger generation beyond the call of duty.

Mr Stone had written his first – well-received – book while serving on a submarine during the war. That romantic beginning coupled with Christopher Wren's room was glamour enough. But there was more – for instance, his battles on the heavily contested fields of seventeenth-century English history.

Another World

And, in my case, there was a uniquely distinguished connection: Redmayne's, the Wigton Tailor. Enter Lawrence Stone in his suit!

Redmayne's specialised in copying suits. Measurements from Oxford and elsewhere were sent up country. The Wigton women's workforce in Redmayne's in Station Road got cracking and back came a replicated suit in practically indestructible material – a dull green tweed. Mr Stone was as tickled by the connection as I was. He even got out of his chair on the first occasion it made itself known to display the dullness and the greenness of the suit. 'So,' he said, 'all things go in circles.' I was ridiculously pleased at the connection. My mother had made buttonholes in that factory, that sweat shop, for seven years . . .

* * *

The undergraduates were given a heavy load. The relationship between supervised teaching and solitary work was dramatically different from what it had been at school. In effect, at Oxford the overwhelming amount of work was homework. But only rarely alone. That was the glitch for me. Unless you could wangle your way to solitary confinement. I found a retreat in a corner of the old Wadham law library. Sometimes Gerald was out of our room but not often enough for the consistency required. There was something attractive about that rather battered library. It resonated centuries of scribal devotion, monks penned in their cells but released to copy commentaries on and illustrate the Gospels, all the way back at the origins of the university.

My favourite segment in the English history course was the post-Roman Celtic Renaissance from the fifth to the eighth centuries in the north, seeded in Iona, flowering largely in Northumbria which at one powerful stage all but took over most of Britain. The added attraction here for me was that the 'almost-conqueror' was called Æthelstan – a combination of my parents' names: Ethel and Stan! And Æthelstan almost made it. But it was the saints and scholars, not the soldiers, who gripped me. It was the period of English history between 412 when the Romans left Britain, to the reign of King Alfred. After that a hop to the Battle of Hastings, all of which, at school, had been bundled through on a couple of Wednesday afternoons.

Now, though, it was given time. Time for Cuthbert and the Celtic monks from Iona and time for Bede to found English history, time for the Holy Island of Lindisfarne, time for Whitby and the power of Hilda and her saintly nuns, time for the warring pagan Vikings to attempt to destroy a divinely layered Christian civilisation of translation and matchless illustration of scripture, the Lindisfarne Gospels, and time for miracles worthy to equal those of the Apostles. Even time to include the seals that frisked around the Farne Islands in the freezing waters the monks endured as their form of self-castigation, believed to bring on sanctity.

Not only had I been to Holy Island and crossed the causeway at the prescribed safe times, but I also knew about the reminders of St Cuthbert all over the north. Particularly, St Cuthbert's churches in the north-west. St Cuthbert's pious influence had inspired Durham Cathedral – a school trip – and York Minster – a visit with Mr Blacker for the York Mystery Plays. Evidence of Celtic Christianity was all over the north, sprung up like dragon's teeth. Not only did I feel territorially proprietorial, I saw my own Christianity in the dusk and then the glow, the light and force of it in the Dark Ages. I wrote a very long essay about that time. 'Go easy,' said Mr Stone, when he had heard out my over-long paean to the Celtic greatness. 'You'll be lucky to get one decent question on this in the entire set of papers. Time to move on.' In a way, I never have. That period, those people, the beginning of the north as such a powerful province and a force is still a homing place.

Of everything on the curriculum in those three years at Oxford, for me this was the crown. These holy men who were also scholars, walking south from the far northern islands, could embrace the faith that gave them such strength and perseverance! They imitated the earlier saints and scholars of Christianity who had sought out solitude in the deserts of the East to find – as they believed – essential isolation for prayer and worship. The sea was the British equivalent of the barren expanse of deserts. Islands were its desert refuges and centres of prayer and scholarship, from the greatness of Lindisfarne to the small island on Keswick Lake on the other side of the country. The core of scholarship at Wadham itself could be seen as a direct descendant of those Celtic monks who walked to Lindisfarne and from there went down the east coast and sailed across the sea to enlighten the Holy Roman Empire.

A Celtic monk of the day wrote a poem which included the lines:

Better far than praise of men
'Tis to sit with book and pen . . .

Chapter Six

Inside the College, I now realise that to some extent I was reconstructing Wigton. The limited space in the College, the small passages and shortcuts, the constant to and fro of the people, the same people day after day on the same routes around the confined place. Gradually, from the window seat as a spectator and then on the ground, I became one of them, or us. I name names and note characteristics as I had done in descriptions of Wigton in the book to which this is a sequel.

It also, I believe, consolidates the strand that aims to be a chronicle, just as its precursor *Back in the Day* will, I hope, be taken not only as an account of my own life but stand as a record of a unique and different period of largely working-class life, its little-appreciated strengths and skills, at a hinge time in the story of England as it moved out of war, empire and world-reaching industry to its more democratic role. It was the body of men and women in the north, in the mills and the mines, in the factories and the sweat shops, which enabled the development of what could be claimed Britain's greatest contribution – the Industrial Revolution. It gave Britain incalculable wealth and changed utterly the pace, the style, the possibility of a greater life here and throughout the world. This was achieved largely by the will, learning and force of 'ordinary' men and women, none of whom had been to university.

Now, after serving its purpose – after not much more than a century – it has been allowed to wither away – unused coal, untouched oil.

It was only after World War I that the names of the majority of such Englishmen were put on public view, on the war memorials in cities, towns and villages. Before this they were numbers: 'and 15 men . . .'

The university world of colleges, libraries, churches, museums and theatres of educated leisure was impossible to herd as neatly as the regiments of working men and women who had made the Industrial Revolution so powerful. I wanted to penetrate this Oxford fortress. I had become addicted to working and walking on my own in Cumbria. This habit persisted. Oxford's side streets and wriggling connections, its open colleges with their imperial variety of gardens, their range of buildings which constantly reminded me of the good fortune of being there and which exuded an atmosphere of being the best place a mind could reach out for, became a drug, as compelling as the Lake District and, like the Lake District, a place with a genius of its own.

When I wandered about I was among strangers but we were all, or mostly, strangers together. Michael said that he had counted more than forty people he had known before he came to Oxford. Old school pals would remain cliques. But to an outsider none of that mattered. Enough men were friendly enough for a common life.

Soon it seemed not all that odd that most of those I passed in the street, or saw in the big libraries, at the lectures and meetings, were young, male and just as self-absorbed as I was. That was the Oxford deal: immersion; now and then we nodded at each other.

I experienced little sense of inferiority in Wadham itself. It was not an issue there – although it may have been in other colleges. It could be seen on the streets if you looked for it. The wooden faces. *Noli me tangere.* There were signs enough. There was a sense that there were those who considered themselves of a higher caste, a better breed, who looked different, set apart, and they were trapped in it. You could see it all about you if you sought it. But it could often be deceptive. Perhaps all of us had been bred to be careful of contact with strangers. 'Never take sweets from a stranger', said an old poster. Yet much of this was ignored – in a rugby team, in a play, in a choir, in a pub; it was just England, All Creatures Great and Small, tentatively adjusting to a new reality.

Of course there were differences. Most of these young men had been packed off to prep school at seven, seconded to public, i.e. private, schools at twelve or thirteen and had grown up in what was a separate country inside our own country. This different country trussed up in traditions and practices was considered to be the ruling tribe. How could it not be? The miracle was that so many of them were easy-going, give-and-take, deeply decent, like Ulick, like Robert or Alan, like Michael . . .

Nevertheless, now and then it was not unlike coming up against a confusingly familiar yet foreign language. That gave it a zest, a taste of adventure, happy to meet each other and then ignore each other. It had an energy. Perhaps all the more energising because of the differences.

It was the preponderance of young men or young gentlemen that was the most intriguing. Where were the young women? They were so few and in such demand. Just as the young gentlemen could be a company, even a regiment, unified in similar tweed jackets, the same sense of neither seeking nor wanting company other than a clique they could always sniff out, so the young women were a breed apart characterised by scarcity. It could seem an alien planet where women had been largely unadmitted, only now and then seen as prospective mates but largely absent in this unique space.

It could be seen as rather genteel science fiction. Women were rarely allowed on board. They were not a block, more of a scattering. A few close companionships denied this. But still so few women. Like others from a similar background I experienced it as an unnecessary absence, an unattractive imbalance. The educational control was decreed overwhelmingly by men, and men traditionally obedient to decades of public chastity, prescriptions of piety and divine order. It said there will forever be this gulf, this separation, the higher (the male) and the lower (the female) and despite biology and the growth of sexual parity in the wider world, this division in my day was still largely observed.

* * *

One Saturday in the first term I made for the Carfax dance hall in the middle of the city. It was just like the County Ballroom in Carlisle, even to the multicoloured spinning ball in the centre of the ceiling. The culture of the room seemed to have been bought at the same shop as the Carlisle version. Same sort of clientele, dominated by the young apprentices from the car industry at Cowley on the edge of town, just as the County had been dominated by apprentices from Cowans and Sheldon, the engineering works in Carlisle. And again a band that aped Glen Miller.

But where was Sarah?

I mooched around and asked for a dance. I got one acceptance – for a quickstep – and two refusals. The girls wanted their friends, the lads from Cowley, or they'd rather settle for each other than this stranger in a clerical grey suit and all the characteristics of a loser. I looked for a phone. Sarah, her father said without any elaboration, was not in. I went back, tried to enjoy the band and failed. Shuffles around in the semi-dark of contented couples were out of reach. Here there were girls who were not in the colleges. I had a comprehensive sensation of being cold-shouldered. Even the girl who had given me the dance had said not a word. I kept her at arm's length, afraid to betray Sarah who was three hundred miles away.

I went out into the street at a mere nine o'clock and took what I thought of as a risk. When I had worked in Paris, before I came to Oxford, I had brooded about strip clubs. Some of the Germans in my new job were on the same scheme as I was. We generally helped out at that large school in the Bois de Vincennes for young foreigners on holiday. Some of the Germans boasted of strip experiences. One night I plucked up courage, in Pigalle, found the cheapest show available – called *Apache* – and went in as if to an appointment with Satan. I felt much the same on that Saturday night in Oxford. There was the Blue Bar. With a reputation. Not all bad. It was not denied that someone in Wadham had met a woman in the Blue Bar and quite soon moved in with her. He was admired for it, especially as it lasted and led to marriage.

On this evening there were two women in one corner chatting, ignoring this hungry new innocent. That was it. I had a pale ale at a distance from the two women. I felt again, as in Paris, that I was supping with the devil. What would I do if one of them came across? One of them looked at me and laughed with her friend. She wore a thick layer of lipstick. She seemed 'so old', nice but old. I swallowed the beer quickly and left, feeling that I had just escaped damnation by a whisker. The only recourse was the pub which was part of Wadham's estate, the King's Arms. I thought I might meet someone I recognised. A table of rugby players. My luck was in. A pint of bitter. The end of a sensational night.

I walked into the College to the sound of party chatter and music coming from some of the rooms. The homesickness which had been kept in check for more than a month burst through. It was a surprise attack. I thought my time in France had seen it off. Not so. Here on a cheerful Oxford Saturday night, it punched into the solar plexus.

* * *

I had planned my next move for some time. I would go to the Banbury roundabout on the Friday evening. Hitch a lift from one of the lorries which went north. Somehow get to Wigton early in the morning and come back after two days. As my tutorial was on Tuesday late afternoon, I could spend two days in Wigton and still be back with the essay for Mr Stone. Get there early Saturday morning. Set off back first thing on Tuesday on the train. Should be possible. Notes for Gerald to give to the scout and the tutor saying that I had an urgent reason to go back north but would return with the essay.

I did not have long to wait at the roundabout. A lorry advertising *Removals* pulled up.

'Can you give us a lift, Mister? I'm going to Carlisle. Well, *near* Carlisle.'

'I'm bound for Wigan.' He was chubby, unshaven, a genial man, with long sideburns. 'I'm likely the best offer you'll get tonight. Hop in.' He helped me in.

'Thank you.'

I offered him a cigarette. I had stepped up the habit in Oxford. The driver reached out with his left arm without taking his eyes off the road, took the cigarette and lit it with a lighter that appeared in his hand as if by magic. He instantly spluttered.

'What's this?'

'It's called Disque Bleu. It's French.'

He coughed heavily and stubbed it out.

'Well, they can keep it. Dear God! French! Have one of mine.'

He offered Capstan Full Strength. My father's favourite. This time I coughed.

He laughed. 'Keep practising,' he said and then, immediately, 'there's a book about Wigan,' he said. 'You'll know about that. You're a student, aren't you?'

I nodded, gasped some more, and sucked once again at the Capstan.

'I can always tell,' he said. 'Soft hands. So what did you make of it?'

'*The Road to Wigan Pier*?'

'That's it. Save there isn't one.'

I let that pass.

'I liked it,' I said. 'I thought he was very honest about coal mining and how hard it was . . .'

'He went down one, didn't he? Credit where it's due. And he was a big tall fella they say. Nearly crippled him.'

'He was trying to find out about working people.'

'I'll give him that.'

'I think those miners were the first English working-class people he'd met,' I said. 'He was very impressed by their politics.'

'I know. I read it. We all read it. Bits of it.'

'Have you read *Animal Farm*? I liked that better.'

We discussed that for some miles.

'Do you play rugby at your university?'

'We do.'

'Why won't your top players take wages for it like we do in the north in the Rugby League?'

'I don't really know. But at school, university, right up to internationals, it's amateur all the way.'

'So they say.' He laughed, and repeated, 'So they say . . . I think it's to do with becoming posher. Like Gentlemen and Players in cricket. All comes down to snobbery. I usually draw in for a pot of tea and a sandwich here . . .'

I tried to pay but he wouldn't hear of it.

* * *

I had a long wait for the lift to Carlisle but once there I got the first bus for Wigton. I had phoned Sarah. She was standing on a bleak empty Market Hill. Her bike leaned against the pub wall. I could have come back safely from a war.

'I told your Mam,' she said. 'She'll have made breakfast.'

I can still sharply remember that arrival, that morning, even that breakfast. In one way it seems too much, that it should have been such a significant encounter. It seemed that the town just surged at me, a wave of recognitions almost swamped my mind. I was back on a firm footing and realised how much I had missed the place and how in its absence I had grown to experience how much it meant.

And its own dialect. A scribbled sign on the word WIGTON at the entrance to the town from Carlisle read, 'Sek a baary laal spot!' What a great little place!

Chapter Seven

Sarah made quick work of breakfast. She had biked into Wigton from Oulton for her Saturday half-day at the bank. We would meet at midday. My mother, having put on a labourer's breakfast, went downstairs from the flat to begin cleaning out the pub and laying the fires in the four rooms. Dad took the opportunity. Sat back. Pulled out the cigarettes – I paused – and then dived in.

'So.' He was so eager, in that moment, in that syllable, I knew more certainly than ever before how much this meant to him. He had largely dammed up his deepest feelings. Now they flew out like a quiverful of arrows. 'So' meant what was it like in that foreign country, the people, the way of life, the opportunities, the newness of that mythical place? I was a messenger from Olympus, transformed since we had last met by the actual experience of having been There, Part of It, that Place above the clouds.

'So!'

I knew what he wanted and I wanted to please him, to thank him, to share this luck of mine and, sentimentally, to let him relish this wholly unanticipated event from the family of his fathers – labourers, coal miners – to his own life denied opportunities, to this, this . . . fairy tale. As he waited – for a moment or two – at the breakfast table, I noticed, as I had done a few times before, the kind and moved look in his eyes, the very slight smile on his lips, which said, 'Who'd have thought it?' 'So!' This said, 'Talk – it's the least you can do.'

'What's the place like?'

I told him as best I could, a rapid skim of the history, the architecture, the gardens, the staircases . . . he nodded, patiently.

'I mean the people,' he said. These were too varied for generalisations but I stumbled on.

'I mean do you feel left out?'

'No.'

That pleased him. To please him further, I added, 'What *you* once said – "you are better than nobody and nobody is better than you".'

He smiled widely and nodded.

'It was a vicar said that. In the forces.'

'And you've passed it on.'

'Do you feel you can keep up?'

'With what?'

'Everything.'

'Well enough.'

'I suppose they're all Tories.'

'No. There's probably as many Labour as Tory. And some Liberals.'

'When you talk about politics, what's your view?'

'Depends.' My father always voted Liberal. In his part of Cumbria the Liberals had been neck and neck with the Conservatives for decades – the Labour Party had struggled. Further to the west coast, the mining area where he came from, it was Labour all the way.

'I'm more for people than parties,' he said. 'I've a great deal of time for Harold Macmillan – what he brought back from the war was a decent understanding of working people. And I liked the way he put it across.'

'Do you think there's what could be called a Ruling Class?' My turn.

'Yes.' He was decisive. 'It's needed. But it shouldn't be set in stone. And it shouldn't just come from one clique. We should shuffle it around. When one clique gets a grip – which it's had in this country for a long time – it can . . . well, we can see it, can't we? It can be, let's say, corrupted. But you have to have somebody in charge and you have to be able to kick them out if they let us down. Do you think there's fair play in this country?'

'No.'

'So what do you and your Oxford friends think about it? Do they try to change it?'

'Some do.' My memory flicked back to the stiff hierarchy of the Oxford Union. 'Maybe not enough, some do. But often it's as if all the important matters have already been sorted out and all that's left is a little adjustment here and there.'

'Do you think there'll be another war and bring in atom bombs?'

That question had been asked at school in debates and religious instruction programmes as well as at my interview for university.

'What I think is this.' I was tentative. 'I can't find a trace of a single powerful deadly weapon in history that has not been used. When we feel we have to use it, we will. So will they – whoever they may be . . .'

And somehow from stumbling we moved to a steadier exchange . . .

* * *

'We'll go to the Legion after I've sorted a few things out.'

First we went down to the cellars.

In the main cellar six barrels were on the ramps.

'I'll deal with these,' he said. 'You carry up. Two pale ale, two milk stout, two Guinness.'

While Dad readjusted the nozzles on the beer barrels, I went into the other cellar and began to shift the crates as I had done for years. There were twenty-four bottles in each wooden crate, handle-grips in the wood at both ends, eleven steps up the staircase. You had to let the crate keep your balance, then along to the bar where the bottles were wiped down, neatly stacked in drill-order lines, labels to the front. I always enjoyed this. I enjoyed working with my father who was so unfussy and meticulous. After he had fixed the barrels he would go back up to the bar and pull through fresh water from the bucket in which he had nozzled the pipes. We said very little to each other. My mother and, at weekends, Mrs Greenop from down the road who helped out would restore the rooms. Dust and clean, make up the fires — the routine did not change.

After the cellar work I would go out into the back and swill out the gents; then to the front, a broad space where the brewers' lorries could park while they offloaded the beer. The front was the only embarrassment. Buses from around the small villages would swing into Market Hill directly opposite the pub, often carrying pupils. If I'd miscalculated the timing, I could be, or felt I was, an object of some derision, especially as my father was strict about the front. Dust and litter had to be swept into the gutter and from there pushed down to the edge of our front and then shovelled up and taken to the dustbins. It was part of

Another World

the job. Three hundred and sixty-five days a year. Opening hours: weekdays 10.30–3.00, 5.30–10.00; Sunday 11.00–2.00, 7.00–10.00.

I liked being part of that, all of us in it together. The pocket money felt earned. There was a hum about it. I had done that every morning. Sometimes in the early evening I would be allowed to serve in the bar – usually more or less empty at that time – while my parents took a break. That was best of all. The feeling of a treat and a breaking of the law.

After breakfast, Sarah went up the street to the bank, from where she would retrieve her bike a few hours later. She would go to Oulton, just over two miles away. I would follow later. She got on very well with my mother, who suggested that after the Carlisle dance in the evening, it might be wiser for Sarah to stay the night in Wigton. That hadn't happened before.

* * *

'We would have time to go to the Legion. There's sure to be a snooker table available.'

'I'm useless at snooker.'

'Here's a chance for some practice.'

As we walked up King Street, the busiest street in the town, I felt as if I were entering a tunnel of warm air being pumped towards my father and me. Though he had not the native hold on the town that marked my mother and myself, his reputation from the aerodrome at Silloth, the factory and the pub, above all his character, had made him well enough known and as easy with the continuous brief greetings as I was.

As we walked up the gentle hill towards the fountain and High Street, I became aware, rather uncomfortably, that there was again something of the proud owner and the show dog about the two of us. When someone approached whose name he thought I might not know he would whisper it in my ear and use it emphatically. Only three times did he say 'he's just nipped back from Oxford' or 'he hasn't changed at all', but undoubtedly a rosette was being put around my neck. It was uncomfortable, but when I glanced at him and saw the pleasure he was getting from this father–son stroll, I tried to dust off any discomfort.

It was not difficult. That gentle stroll up the street released a swarm of memories and recognition – Smith's vast clothing shop; the Spotted Cow snack bar where William sometimes worked to help his father, as George Johnston did three doors up in a boot and shoe shop that had been set up by a George Johnston in the 1840s and continued with George Johnstons ever since. Ronnie's the barber with his parting shot to the adults as they left ('Anything for the weekend, sir?'), the copies of *Tit-Bits* neatly stacked beside the fire. Noel Carrick across the street, a Roman Catholic whose nephew was training to be a priest; the Co-op; the hardware store where Michael Saunderson worked for *his* father at weekends, on they went, these shops, as if graven into the place from its first planting by the Vikings . . .

* * *

I wondered why I had left Wigton. Surely there was life enough here and hereabouts. The fells just a few miles away, the richness of old experiences now being revivified despite my absence at university. How many of those of us who had pulled up our roots could not have regretted it from time to time? Perhaps this, an early visit, was the most vulnerable time or perhaps it was just a quirk in my nature, like the poet John Clare's inability to function after moving a mile or two from one village to another. Whatever, it swept me back and swept back feelings stronger than any so far registered in Oxford...

Dad arranged the snooker balls at one end of the table in a triangular frame which left them perfectly formed and just waiting to be disrupted. He let me take the first shot. I felt an adult as I banged the white ball down the table and scattered the neat regiment to the walls.

The Legion was barely half full. We were the only table in operation. This enabled my father to give me a lesson. How to hold the cue, how to chalk the tip of it, how to use the slightly raised sides of the table to bounce away the ball to cunning effect.

He was a good teacher. It is no boastful modesty to confess that I was no good at the game, even for a beginner. As I was a no-good beginner with darts in the pub. With all the advantages of having the darts room to myself for practice on weekend afternoons, when it came to the games I was always and effortlessly outclassed. Still, I played snooker with my father on that Saturday morning and it was good.

* * *

Sarah had left for home by the time I went to meet her at the bank. We had agreed that she would come to Wigton later in the afternoon, leave her bike and her change of clothes at my place, and we would walk down to the station with the others for the Carlisle train.

The walk up the town with my father had been disturbing. The Oxford weeks had not been successful in replacing the past. To my surprise, I telephoned my old headmaster, Mr Stowe. I'd thought of doing so a few times at Oxford but now, with a free afternoon, it seemed the best chance I would get.

He was in the house and yes, I could pop up at around three. The plunge into the town had given me the nerve to do what I had tentatively sketched out over the past few weeks.

Why did I want to be at university? Why did I intend to leave a place, a people, a past that suited me so happily? I could get a starter job in local government or go down to the factory to work in the accounts department or even get taken on as a junior in one of the solicitors' offices – such jobs had been taken by boys in the years ahead of me at school. The library had moved from the yard in which we had lived to the Quaker Meeting House where there were far more books. There were the swimming baths, a drama society, the AYPA, a choir, maybe a chance to make the second team rugby . . . friends who I currently assumed would be lifelong; and Sarah of course.

What was the point?

Almost in a daze, as if the walk through the town had revealed and fortified a hitherto buried plan, I had made the call to Mr Stowe.

It was a miserable day. Steady drizzle. A wind getting up, swaying the massive chestnut trees in the auction field. Few people in the damp streets. Yet I could not think of a better place to spend a life.

Mr Stowe was as brisk and incisive as ever he had been teaching us French and religious instruction. He had been

Another World

brought up by a Methodist preacher, his father, in the town of Aspatria, eight miles from Wigton, a town which had connections with the Celtic saints, the Roman army and rugby. In the war he had become a major in intelligence after winning a scholarship to Oxford from the school of which he was now headmaster – and at which he stayed until his retirement, radical in his determination to straighten out and inspire what had been a rather drowsy grammar school. When I got to his house, up the long drive between the school fields and the vicarage, there was a moment before I rang the bell when I thought I ought to think better of it. But by coming to see him, I had thought better of it.

After my apologies for bothering him and his reassurances that it was no trouble, we went to the drawing room of the substantial Victorian house where he pointed out where I should sit as I looked at the wall of photographs of the town and the school and the county and the army, photographs which were mixed in with snaps of the local bird life taken on his regular walks along the nearby coast.

On cue, Mrs Stowe brought in a tray: two cups, tea, a plate of biscuits and a cut cake, gingerbread. Then she left us to it. There was a fire, logs neatly stacked beside it. The sound of the fire seemed rather loud. Mr Stowe offered me a cup of tea and an empty plate on which – it had all become slow motion – I was invited to place a slice of gingerbread.

For a few moments I forgot what had led me there.

He waited. My silence provoked platitudes: was I enjoying Oxford was the key question. To which I had no conclusive answer. Yes and no was unsatisfactory, however true.

It was not a time to waste Mr Stowe's time.

Outside, a wind was driving gusts of noise that provided a rather comforting backup to the crackling of the fire. I felt that I had turned up to hear what punishment was due. The Methodist minister in the man set in front of me came to the end of his polite silence.

'I presume you have concerns about Oxford.'

'Well, sir . . . yes . . . yes, I do.'

'It can be an unaccommodating environment. I was lucky to have been in the army before I got there. The gap between school – it was a boys' school then – and university was bridged by military service. We had little or no choice about anything, which at the time I found very comforting.' He smiled. 'We had no time to think about our position. It was all done for us. I suspect your generation doesn't have that.' He paused. I stalled. Mr Stowe showed no irritation. The booming of the wind took over the sound of the room.

'I think I might have done the wrong thing.'

'Not uncommon. Especially after the second term. I assume you'll pass your Prelims. There's a sense that you'll be locked in for the three years after that.' He must have seen how uncomfortable I was. He topped up my cup and then he fell silent.

I was on.

'There's plenty to like,' I said, 'people, places, just being with so many my age in a college as friendly as Wadham. But . . .' He had decided to let me do this on my own. 'But . . . I'm not sure what I'm doing there. I only went because Mr James thought it was a good idea to put me in for the exams. I enjoyed taking them. But that was more to please him. My parents were happy enough but they set no great store by it. My mother certainly would have preferred me to stay in Wigton, in time get married here and have a family. I was very happy with my friends, what they were doing, and how close we were together. Oxford was a bit like Albania.' Mr Stowe smiled. 'Seriously foreign, as if I'd been expelled to another country for a crime I didn't commit. And now I'm there, and wherever I look it's good – well, there are some obvious trip wires – but when I come back here I know where I am. I feel I know every bit of it and with good reason – because it's a place that has a mixture in it, craftsmen and women, gardeners, carpenters, factory workers, decorators, lawyers, teachers, bus drivers, shopkeepers, people who've been here or their families have for generations, some struggling, all sorts and shapes and sizes, not uniform – not at all like the elite battalion feeling that is the core of the regiment of Oxford. Even though some people' – I thought of Robert, Ulick, Michael and Alan – 'are as good as it gets, but . . .'

Mr Stowe was sufficiently experienced to take my stumbling seriously. He took his own line. 'There are some boys who come to this school from nearby villages,' he began, 'only six or seven miles away – Caldbeck for instance, or Bolton or Ireby; even those from the two larger towns, Silloth and Aspatria, where I came from, and they express much the same as you are doing now – moving those few miles tears up their roots, sometimes so deep that they can never settle. I suspect you may be one of those. Nothing can replace what you once were. It's pulling up the deep past you have developed and cultivated and now discover you don't want to lose.'

He was right.

'I could have a good life here,' I said, more firmly than I had said anything so far. 'It's just a waste of money me staying on at Oxford.'

'Have you talked to your parents?'

'No. Not yet.'

'And Mr James?'

'I know what he would say. And I would feel I had let him down.'

'When did this decision come to you?'

'It's been brewing for some time.'

'I believe that.' He paused. 'What is it? "You can take the boy out of Wigton but you can't take Wigton out of the boy."'

'Some manage,' I said. 'Some say they can't wait to get out of their town.'

'The best I can do is to advise you to give it more time. You worked in Paris for the Abbé Pierre. I remember the talk you gave on that when you came back – very interesting too. You went away with the Scouts to Iona as I remember . . .'

'This is different. This is for life.'

Mr Stowe smiled.

'Life has a way of sorting itself out,' he said. 'I suggest you give it until the end of the academic year. Do the exams next term – pass them! – then there's the summer term and my view is that by then you'll be well bedded in.'

There was an authoritative finality in the headmaster's words. There had been no reference to the fact that this discussion had been prompted by my reunion with Sarah.

When I told her about it later, as we walked down Station Road to catch the train to Carlisle – there would be about a dozen of us making for the dance at the County Ballroom – Sarah simply said, 'That would be giving up.'

It was the pin that pricked the balloon. The headmaster's parting words had been 'I think you owe it to Mr James'.

* * *

The dance in Carlisle in a ballroom identical in appearance to that on Carfax corner in Oxford was chalk and cheese, friendly replacing frigid. And Sarah and I still breathed in the memory of that Saturday not so long ago when the Memphis Five: Tich Parker on double bass (a tea chest, a broomstick and thick twine, surprisingly effective in providing a bass beat); Eric Hetherington on a small side drum and a substantial washboard; Paul Allotson and Robert Wilson on guitars; my effort at the mic imitating Lonnie Donegan. Not a great success, but as one of the band told us afterwards, 'You'll get better. It's the only way it can go.'

Lemonade at the interval, and later a stroll across the car park to the railway station and the empty train waiting in a lonely bay to transport metropolitan adventurers west, a coach to ourselves for a delicious spell and, finally, Wigton, back to the by now closed pub – time in the kitchen where those who had helped out enjoyed free drinks and we listened to the history of the pub's Saturday night. No fights, a packed singing room, the carefully ordered bottles swiftly depleted, a fug of smoke. Two bonneted and black-uniformed women from the Salvation Army came in to sell the *War Cry*. They got a courteous reception.

* * *

Sarah went through my bedroom to hers, long vacated and now primped up by my mother, a glass of flowers on a side table.

When the pub was reduced to silence and even the streets seemed abandoned, as quietly as I could, I went into Sarah's room and into her bed and after a while fell asleep, until at early dawn both of us were violently woken up by my mother's 'STANLEY!'

Breakfast was awkward. 'We trusted you,' my mother said. My father nodded and went down to the cellar. I followed to help him replenish the Saturday shelves. Dad's policy was silence on the matter. As the two of us biked out to her home in Oulton, Sarah said that there had been very little conversation in the kitchen after Dad and I had left.

We agreed not to meet the next morning. I would catch the earliest train to Carlisle, from there across country to Oxford.

'I'm glad you made the effort,' she said as we paused outside the farm.

'It was great.'

Sarah laughed.

'Well. It had its moments. Let's put it that way.'

'It was really good to see you,' she said, with unaccustomed feeling.

We hugged each other as if for the last time.

Then I left, swung down the hill, past the dense forest, the road to myself, then uphill to Standingstone, Wigton below laid out like a tapestry, street lights, house lights, back home.

Chapter Eight

The next time I made it up to Cumbria, Sarah and I went for the inevitable bike ride. We headed for Bassenthwaite Lake. The Pheasant, an old coaching inn, stood a few yards from the lakeside, which sheltered a small station for boats. In the middle of the lake there were some white-sailed yachts moving, stately, slowly in the light breeze, like swans. We hired a rowing boat. The Skiddaw range of fells reared up behind them providing protective comfort. It was easy to lock in the oars and drift.

'It's a bit strange.'

'It's like memory lane.'

'But not quite.'

'No.' Sarah smiled and nodded. And then, with visible effort, she added, 'I've missed seeing you.'

From Sarah, such declarations were few. This was said with unusually strong feeling.

'Me too,' was the best I could manage. I wanted to say that only now, in this moment, did I fully feel us together and begin to thaw out. 'I think I've only been pretending to enjoy Oxford. There's plenty to do. And good people. But . . .'

The separation still lay between us.

'It isn't anywhere like the same,' she concluded. And smiled. 'For me neither.'

'I keep thinking it wasn't worth it.'

'I'm sure it is. It is.' Sarah spoke emphatically. 'We'll get through it. In no time you'll be back for Christmas.'

Why could I not find anything as cheerful and helpful? I said nothing. The boat lifted and swayed from side to side. Across the lake there was a small church which looked snug beside the water.

'Let's go and look.'

I picked up the oars and went across to what proved to be St Bega's. The church had been founded on a sixth-century Celtic hermit site. Inside the tiny building there was information about St Bega, an Irish princess who had escaped across the Irish sea to what became known as St Bees, and drifted down county until she found a spot, then an island, where she established a nunnery and, it was claimed, brought about miracles. In the middle of that same lake, an information sheet said, Tennyson, while he was staying with a local scholar, had written the passage in his King Arthur poem in which an arm came out of the waters holding the great sword Excalibur. We pulled the boat up onto the shore and walked along the lakeside path looking for a place, which we found, and our lives reconnected. I rowed back slowly, savouring the pace, the return of what had been so strong and happy about our past.

A pub lunch in the bar in which I'd had my first drink. A clumsy game of billiards in a nearby room. Not wanting to touch each other. Unable to leave each other alone. Dawdling back to Wigton and then on to Oulton a couple of miles away where Sarah lived . . .

I got on with my essay the next day while Sarah was at work in the bank. There was time enough to walk around Wigton again which was like drifting through a familiar art gallery. Across Market Hill, up the steps to Birdcage Walk, to Arnison's, the lemonade factory in which I'd worked in the summer. Down Little Lane to the crossroads. On to Kirkland, or head for Highmoor House with its high Venetian tower? Then Brindlefield, across to South End by way of Brackenlands and into the Showfield, from there along to Park House where my grandparents lived in an atmosphere of unchangedness . . .

We went to the pictures on Monday. I biked back to Oulton with Sarah to our favourite place in the barn. The next morning I caught the first bus to Carlisle and then a couple of connections to Oxford in time for the tutorial. I finished my essay on the train.

Oxford seemed to be rather a dry place, more a theatre than a city, a spectacle rather than a habitation.

'Everything okay in the north?'

Mr Stone was amused. I nodded and prepared to read the essay.

'Wigton?'

'Yes, sir.'

'I forgot to ask. What did your mother do in that clothing factory? In Redmayne's.'

'She made buttonholes.'

He was impressed.

'For seven years,' I said. 'Until she got married, which meant that she had to leave.'

'Good Lord . . .' His smile was generous. 'Buttonholes . . .'

I began to read my essay to a man who knew so much more about it than I ever would, a man chained to this routine while his own work was straining for attention, a man impressed by buttonholes.

Chapter Nine

While I'd been in the Legion, my Aunt Ada had come into the pub. On most Saturdays she came to Wigton to do the bulk of a week's shop. She always concluded the trip by coming to see my mother. Her sister.

My mother never admitted this to me – the stigma at that time was as rigid as a Commandment.

They had the same mother, Belle. My mother, Ethel, was fostered by Mrs Gilbertson; Geoff's mother, Ada, went to Mrs Blair, who lived in a small house in the Stampery, a cluster of rather isolated homes in a field near the railway line. She had a lodger, Johnny King, who was a cutter at the Redmayne's clothing factory. He was deaf and dumb; consequently, Mrs Blair and all of us close to her picked up the deaf-and-dumb finger alphabet. Ada and Ethel not only looked like sisters, in one photo they might have been twins. They knew of each other from childhood but nothing was said.

The pub was conveniently opposite the bus station. Ada had to have her back 'seen to'; once a fortnight she went to the house of Mr Wood, part-time bookie and amateur masseur. She then caught a bus back to Fletchertown, the village about six miles away towards the fells where she lived with her husband Silas and my cousins, her five children, all boys. Geoffrey, Brian, Peter,

Colin and Robin. They were as much a family for me as for each other.

***

So far the two books, *Back in the Day* and this one, have settled on Wigton, c.1939–1954 – childhood, adolescence, the intricate tapestry of a small northern town, Norse in original settlement, grown to be a thriving market town of about five thousand people – several churches and chapels, a dozen pubs, schools, two successful factories, some dozen shops, clubs, sports centres from swimming to rugby, to football, tennis, bowls – England in a nutshell.

This book moved to Oxford as its hub, dozens of colleges, a magnificent centre of learning, a world centre of academic excellence, a life that still held to its mediaeval character, steadily embracing new sciences and honouring the traditions of centuries. While Wigton was sufficient to itself save for expeditions into the nearby Lake District, its fells and rivers, waterfalls and the Lakes themselves, Oxford spun out to Europe, to entering politics, to institutions preparing lives for the Church, the law, scholarship, politics, journalism . . . it was another world.

But there is yet another place, the one I left behind, the world of the northern working class with the skills and application which had brought it astounding advances in engineering and manufacturing. A place which could fairly be called the backbone of the country. A place as distinctive as Oxford and Wigton. To overlook it would be to strip this account of its completeness.

***

Geoff, a couple of years older than me, the oldest of the boys, was always a hero. We looked alike, save he was leaner and always fitter. He had been given boxing lessons by a retired pro in an adjacent village and, to quote his proud brother Brian, 'Geoff was never beaten at his own weight. He was very quick.' He was a featherweight. The problem was that he was so good they kept putting him in with heavier men. It was his spirit that kept him in the game. My father liked and admired him as much as I did. Geoff would come to Wigton to stay with us, head to tail in my single bed, first bus back to Fletchertown in the morning. The outing enabled us to go to Carlisle covered market to see the boxing. My father was keen. He had got hold of a big pair of puffed sparring gloves and Geoff would practise on me in the back yard. 'How's he doing?' my father would ask Geoff. 'He's game,' said Geoff. 'I'll give him that.' The truth was Geoff could have felled me with one hand tied behind his back.

He did his National Service in the RAF in Germany, where any chance of a settled career ended when, drunk, he 'decked' a sergeant who tried to arrest him for disorder. Geoff's usual drink – orange juice – had been spiked with a heavy measure of vodka by his friends. No excuses were acceptable. It finished his career in the RAF.

He went to the fire brigade in the Midlands. To hear him talk about controlling a leaping fire once you were inside a burning building was to hear a detailed lecture about taking serious risks to his own life to help people he had never met. He was and remains more like a brother than a cousin.

Brian was the second brother – almost exactly my age. He was as tough as an oak door. He worked in the town of

Aspatria, five miles from Fletchertown, in a firm which made mattresses. The daily lifting and handling of these bulky objects had built up outstanding strength. I went to Aunty Ada's on many a Saturday evening to get out of the pub in its noisiest phase. I would wrestle with Brian in the sitting room while Aunty Ada sat on a small stool, hunched up to the fire, ignoring the action, intently reading a magazine, *exactly* as my mother did. Brian always won our fights, which meant that he pinned my shoulders down on the floor so that I couldn't move and I had to give in.

Brian enjoyed fighting. When it was serious, the fight would be arranged in one of the sheep pens, gates locked, shirts off. Bare fists. All of us went to a dance one night in an aircraft hangar at Kirkbride. Dad had worked there in a reserved occupation as a fitter. When the war started, damaged planes would hedge-hop from Kent to Kirkbride, isolated on the Solway, many miles from any city centre or industrial conurbation and considered to be safe from German bombers. Dad joined up a few months into the war. After 1945, the hangars at Kirkbride were harnessed for various enterprises – one as a space for dances.

Later on, when I was about to go to university, I went to a dance there again with Geoff and Brian. A fight erupted. We all but sprinted across the floor to join the fast-gathering ring of spectators. It seemed to me that Brian was looking for a chance to join in. He was. He explained this gravely when we went back to our table. 'It might have been somebody we knew,' he said, 'and he might have needed a hand.' With scarcely a heartbeat of a pause he said to me, very affectionately, 'Why don't we go outside for a fight now? Just you and me.'

'You'll murder me! I've gone soft.'
'You were always up for it.'
'That was back then.'

Geoff tapped Brian's shoulder, I remember that clearly. Just a light tap. 'Leave him be,' he said. He did.

Brian's real passion was for the theatre. The village of Fletchertown, about six hundred houses at that time, had a Dramatic Society. It was one of my Aunt Ada's hobbies, and photos show her in several productions, often next to Brian, who went one further and wrote sketches for the company.

My mother was a little in awe of her sister's accomplishments. As well as the theatre, Ada was expert in her minute knowledge of nature, which my mother enjoyed looking at, but her knowledge of the natural world was patchy.

'And five boys!'

Peter, the next in line after Brian, worked in the main Wigton factory all his life, and was captain of the darts team at the Apple Tree at Mealsgate, the nearest pub to the dry Methodist Fletchertown. There were three shifts at the factory: 6 a.m. to 2 p.m., 2 p.m. to 10 p.m., 10 p.m. to 6 a.m. Every week a different shift. It was not an easy servitude. Colin, the next in line, went on to work worldwide on oil rigs. He came and lived with us in Wigton at one time. Robin, the youngest, had a nasty accident when he was a child, all but drowned in the swimming pond the older boys had made for themselves by damming up the River Ellen. There was little chance he would be able to work full-time, but he insisted he wanted to try. Brian got him a light job in the mattress factory in Aspatria. They travelled there and back together. In the early days some bullying went on.

Brian got to the bottom of it and 'had a word' with the culprits. They let Robin be after that.

Save for Robin, they did the work that made the world go round. Yet they were destined over a few generations to change from the Essential Working Class to the forgotten majority.

It was impossible not to compare it with Oxford, the one bred by and for privilege, scholarship, favourable opportunities emanating from a historically successful traditional education, the other bred from efforts of the white working class in the Industrial Revolution which enriched this country more than anything before or since. I heard little complaint. The whole hierarchy was propped up largely by the tolerance of those who bent themselves to accept the harder path and enhanced it by their skills and the discovery of talents which opportunity provided. They created a working-class culture which grew so powerful it was felt that it had to be tamed.

What Fletchertown had provided for almost a hundred years was work in the coal mines. Fletchertown was built on coal located under rock half a mile or so south of what became the village.

The Fletcher brothers who opened up the mines with the help of investment by three local landowners were fortunate to be able to link up with an intricate railway system but unlucky initially in failing to find a sufficient local workforce. So they built one for themselves: Fletcher's Town – Fletchertown – to service the mines.

At first they built houses in what became West Street, followed by North and South Streets, Quarry Street, in which the Hocking family lived, and Skiddaw Terrace, named after the most northerly of the fells which could be clearly seen just beyond the new small town. This was in the late nineteenth century. The streets were mud and ash, the terraced houses were brick and well built. There was a back yard which held the WC, the washhouse and the coalshed. You walked straight into a small kitchen and from there into a living room in which we ate, wrestled, played board games and failed to perturb Aunty Ada reading on her small stool in front of the fire. The bedroom options somehow absorbed us. There was a loft, which helped out. Many people had big families – up to six in one instance. People had to 'manage'. One treat for me was that I was allowed to wear long trousers way before Wigton ways allowed them – hand-me-downs from Geoff.

By the 1950s, when I began to go to Fletchertown quite frequently on Saturday late afternoons to return by the last bus which got to Wigton just before closing time or, preferably, to stay over for the night, the houses were allowed to decline. The suggestions to pull the lot down met with protests from the families who had lived there for three or four generations. Eventually grants were secured, leaseholds were put up for sale at competitive prices and people like Geoff's parents began to buy the properties which they restored at their own expense. Fletchertown endured.

For a place whose primary resource had been coal mines, it grew to upwards of a thousand inhabitants.

There was a men's cricket team which did well in the local league and, more successfully, a women's cricket team which swept the board. A thriving Boy Scouts troop was set up. There was a choir at the Methodist chapel. A small proportion of children took and won scholarships to the two Wigton grammar schools, Nelson's School for Boys and the Thomlinson Girls' School.

We played street games in barely lit streets – chasey, a form of tag, games I'd been brought up on in Wigton but here given more edge by the comparative modesty of the number of hiding places. There was a Co-op, a few shops, a post office and the school, which doubled as a social centre. There was a snooker room under the memorial hall – no charge.

Much of the information I have about life in Fletchertown has been gathered from Geoff. But another aspect of this village was the strong affection it drew from those who lived there and their determination to write down what they saw and appreciated about the place in which they lived. There are up to a dozen booklets, some more than thirty pages, illustrated with photographs of people and houses, lists, local history. A remarkable assembly for such a small place. Fletchertown, from its installation as a mining village, evoked curiosity and affection and these booklets confirm that they wanted it to be known beyond their own time.

The book I refer to in the following paragraphs was 'researched, compiled and printed' in 2009, as the title page tells us, by Mick James, who lived at No. 5 Front Street. I was given permission to quote whatever I needed.

The shoal of mines found at Mealsgate in the Parish of Allhallows, about half a mile from Fletchertown, was activated by the Fletcher brothers, who became rich, went into Parliament and befriended George Moore, a local philanthropist whose CV closely imitates that of Dick Whittington. Moore went to London lured by talks of golden pavements,

Another World

failed to find them, went up Highgate Hill, heard the London bells ring out, 'Turn again, Whittington, Lord Mayor of London', which he did and which he became. George Moore similarly went to London to seek his fortune, found it and returned to Cumberland, bought the mansion of Whitehall, a few hundred yards downhill from Fletchertown, and became not only its prime benefactor, with scholarships for the children who had passed exams but whose parents could not afford to keep them, but also paid for over a thousand weddings. This set an example for others, the Lawsons of Braithwate, for instance, who felt obliged to follow suit.

Using the research from this book, I want to give some indication of Fletchertown's past and its mining history which is characteristic of the British industrial experience so opulent in material rewards for the whole country and eventually the world, such an example of human guts and skills, such an unnecessary victim in its decline. It was in its generation a heroic phase. None of those involved in the origin of the Industrial Revolution went to grammar school or university – so what do we conclude from that? The least to be said is that the university contributed to the running of the country in its more traditional Establishment spheres but contributed very little to its economic development on any scale that could have brought benefit to the masses. The Industrial Revolution – a university of technology – brought out hitherto buried skills from people who would have characterised themselves as 'just ordinary'. It developed remarkable competence, and even genius, a genius that the world copied and from which a new world emerged. This was done at high cost to those who actually did the work, and these, the miners, are commemorated in the book to which I refer. Although they could be called a small part in what became a global revolution, their story can be dug out of this small settlement of Fletchertown, 100 per cent characteristic of its kind, dug in as the graves were dug in as a result of continuously perilous work. Allhallows Mine was sunk between Mealsgate and Fletchertown by the Fletcher brothers to a thirty-inch seam at sixty-five fathoms. They gave their name to this intricate under-earth factory.

There were haulage men, shifters, packers, brushers, putters, onsetters – shiftmen – on goes the list of distinct and indispensable jobs where a slip could and did lead to death.

I pick out the hewers partly because so many met their death, partly because a childhood friend in Wigton was surnamed Hewer and from that I see it branded into the area and I want to develop what this occupation entailed. It seems to me to be central. Mick James spares no details. The following lists are taken from his book. To repeat them as faithfully as they were recorded seems to me to be the clearest way to say: this is their book.

> 1825. A Hewer is one who hews or cuts coal from its natural situation. His usual wages (1849) are from 3s 9d to 4s 3d per day of eight hours working and his average employment four or five days in the week. He also has, as part of his wages, a house containing two or three rooms, according to the number of his family, and a garden of which the average size might be six or eight perches; also a measure of small coals each fortnight for the loading of which he pays sixpence.

1892. A Hewer is the actual coal digger. Whether the seam be so thin that he can hardly creep into it on hands and knees or whether it be thick enough for him to stand upright he is the responsible workman who loosens the coal from the bed. The Hewers are divided into 'fore-shift' and 'back-shift' men. The fore usually work from four in the morning until ten and the latter from ten until four. Each man works one week in the 'fore-shift' and one week in the 'back-shift' alternately. Every man on the 'fore-shift' marks 3 on his door. This is the sign for the 'caller' to wake him at that hour. When roused by that functionary he gets up and dresses in his pit clothes, which consist of a loose jacket, vest and knee breeches, all made of thick white flannel, long stockings, strong shoes and a close-fitting thick leather cap. He then takes a piece of bread and water, or a cup of coffee, but never a full meal. Many prefer to go to work fasting. With a tin bottle full of cold water or tea, a piece of bread which is called his 'bait', his Davy lamp and 'baccy box' he says goodbye to his wife and speeds off to work. Placing himself in the cage, he is lowered to the bottom of the shaft where he lights his lamp and proceeds 'in by' to a place appointed to meet the deputy. This official examines each man's lamp and, if found safe, returns it locked to the owner. Each man then finding from his deputy that his place is right, proceeds onward to his place, his pick in one hand, his lamp in the other. He travels thus a distance varying from one hundred to six hundred yards. Sometimes the roof under which he has to pass is not more than three feet high. To progress in this space the feet are kept wide apart, the body is bent at right angles with the hips, the head is held well down and the face is turned forward. Arrived at his place, he undresses and begins by hewing out about fifteen inches of the lower seam. He thus undermines it and the process is called 'kirving'. The same is done up the sides. This is called 'nicking'. The coal thus hewn is called small coal, and that remaining between the kirve and the nicks is the 'jud' or top which is either displaced by driving in wedges or is blasted down with gunpowder. It then becomes 'the rounding'. The Hewer fills his tubs and continues thus hewing and lifting.

Shifters. 1825. Men who repair horse ways and other passages in the mines and keep them free from obstruction.

Brusher. 1894. Person employed to cut or blast the roof or floor of a roadway so as to give more height.

Deputies. 1849. A set of men employed in setting timber for the safety of the workmen; they also draw the props in the working from the places where they are no longer required for further use . . .

The industry below ground was as complex as the industry coal sustained above ground. All of the above was carried out in the small coalfield of Fletchertown until it ceased to be productive.

The fatal casualties in that small coalfield were indicative of the numbers lost throughout the coalfields of the UK. Sometimes in massive accidents – my grandfather survived one of these – often involving children. Here in the small Fletchertown mine is a compressed list of the hewers who lost their lives. There were ten different jobs but the hewer

Another World

was face to face with the coal. Here is a taste of the deaths over a few decades.

> Bell, Richard. 30 May 1900 aged 28. Fall of stone.
> Brown, Wilfred. Oct. 1899 aged 27.
> Buchanan, Joseph. 16 Sept. Fall of stone. Aged 18.
> Cass, Joseph. 09 Dec. 1913. Aged 39.
> Davidson, Isaac. 03 Sept. 1878. Fall of stone.
> Jones, William. 23 June 1907. Aged 39.
> Lessater, Christopher. 22 Feb. 1881. Aged 35. Fall of coal.
> Lawman, William. 23 June 1893. 24. Fall of large stone.
> Lightfoot, Thomas. 23 Sept. 1885. Aged 55. Fall of roof.
> Lowther, William. 02 Oct. 1913. Aged 28. A burst from the roof.
> O'Neal, Martin. 13 March 1906. Fall of stone.
> Scott, Archibald. 18 July 1908. Aged 53. Crushed against door frame by engine set.

And there were deaths to packers, brushers, putters, onsetters, roller-way men . . .

* * *

This is one mark of the intensity of life as lived in even the smallest coalfield. More evidence comes from the listings supplied by Mick James and the team. The listings are a compact encyclopaedia of what was no more than a small village of a few hundred houses.

In these lists Fletchertown shows its range, ingenuity and determination to construct civic variety on what had been an uninhabited rock.

There was a school, with six teachers – for singing, art, P.T., domestic science, woodwork; a separate infants school; sixty-three boys and fifty-five girls aged five to fifteen.

A list of the travelling shops and salesmen who visited the parish: twenty-one. Food supplies produced in Great Britain and sold in the village: thirteen. Food in local shops from temperate lands: seven. From the Tropics: twenty.

A football club, two cricket clubs, one for men the other for women, darts, a pigeon club, a billiard room. A few miles away a swimming pool, tennis, a rugby club, a bowls club.

A chapel (Methodist), a church (C of E), a library.

Plant life, from chestnut trees to oak, beech, ash, holly, elderberry, hazel nut.

Flowers: where found, flower month, height, food value. From buttercups to marigolds, dog roses, primroses, foxgloves, hyacinths.

And a similar itemising intensity applied to animals: from rabbits to foxes, hares, badgers, weasels, stoats – where seen and their habitats.

A list of birds with beautiful plumage, from cock pheasants through goldcrests, starlings, swifts, chaffinches – fifteen in all.

Another category was local birds protected by law – from seagulls to owls, kestrel hawks, racing pigeons.

And then the songster birds – skylark, blackbird, thrush.

Birds that eat flesh, birds that are helpful to the farmer.

Listed and printed by Mick James – showing that however small in size and often struggling in material, this tiny spot of the map was rich, varied and cherished often beyond credibility.

On all levels it could match anybody.

Perhaps it is not too romantic to believe that the scrupulous dedication to each aspect of the work bred its workers with the confidence and expertise to reconstruct houses, build schools and chapels and memorial halls – construct a world above ground which would be, in its own way, as carefully cultivated as that below and form a variegated, robust community.

It would be fascinating if it were possible minutely and accurately to chart and compare the longer term of the advantage given to society by someone who hewed coal and someone who read classics at Oxford, someone who understood and fought fire and someone who grappled with physics, a community which changed civilisation and a community which preserved it.

* * *

The allotments were the lungs and often the glory of such villages as Fletchertown.

In 1917 two one-acre plots of ground on the edge of Fletchertown were leased by a local landowner for use as allotments by the people of the village. The war was on. This move aimed to help feed the population.

Geoff's father, my Uncle Silas, was one who seized on it.

Silas had been adopted and fostered in Wigton along with his older sisters. Wigton attracted Travellers and fair people, especially in winter to see them through. In milder weather they toured in the north with entertainments that beguiled Silas, who, aged fourteen, for reasons not wholly clear, joined a Traveller family and stayed with them for two years. He left them at sixteen 'with a bit of a pay-off', according to Geoff, enlisted as a boy soldier and stayed in the army for sixteen years. 'He was very careful with his money,' says Geoff, 'and when he came out and back to Wigton he bought a small French car which got him going.'

The car took him to Fletchertown after he had met and married Ada in Wigton. It also equipped him to drive a post office van into the hills behind Skiddaw in the mornings, where he delivered mail to small, widely spread communities, and then put in time so that he could return to the letter boxes and collect the mail that would have been posted an hour or two after midday and take it to Wigton. To fill in the time he got permission from a local landowner to rebuild a hut in the woods. He had a stove, a fire, a mattress, an old chair. He would camp there, fish in the small lake nearby, Over Water, and make up for the sleep denied him on the previous night. Then he would set off back to Wigton with the afternoon post.

After three years in the army, Silas decided to join the band. They wanted recruits and he was taught to play the cornet. He got the knack for it quite soon and spent much of the rest of his army life being happily shifted from place to place with one of the army bands. By the time he was demobbed – before the Second World War – he had developed a yen to settle down. The post office job was perfect. Ada was ten years his junior and they seem to have been very contented as a couple. Silas was accustomed to order and loyalty. That house which could be rumbustious when the indoor play threatened to take over would calm down in a trice when he bid the family to stop. His family was strictly obedient and, considering the differences between the boys, harmonious. I presume that years in the army as a boy and young man taught him how to manage. He was law and order cloaked under tolerance and humour. And there was the cornet. For a man who had led a colourful life he was rather quiet, with a twinkle rather than a laugh, average height, very strong and a man who made good friends across those bleak northern fells where the living was not easy.

Silas's 'treasure' was his allotment. He had taken on one of the largest lots and cultivated it with rosette-winning zealotry disguised as 'just getting on with it'.

Geoff worked with him more often than all the others. Brian and Peter helped out, as did Colin when asked to lend a hand; Robin pottered around the hen pens. But Geoff, the oldest, was, and was expected to be by his father, full on. After school, it was down to the allotment. I went a few times and found it impossible to be anything but a spectator. Silas and Geoff had it too well sorted out to tolerate the interposition of an amateur and they could see I would never have the heart or the head or the diligence for it.

The allotment looked as trim as a crack platoon on the parade ground.

I asked Geoff to take me through it. The allotment would feed the family, help out one or two other families and, at Christmas, make money. As time went on, Silas acquired extra land.

Geoff took me down to the allotment. 'Starting with the vegetables,' he said, 'to be fresh on the plate every day if possible. We had potatoes old and new, carrots, sprouts, turnips, swedes, beetroot, cabbage, spring onions and Spanish onions, rhubarb, runner beans, peas that wound up the stakes, all kept tip-top and drilled in rows that would have competed with the Household Guard. Over there were a couple of Russet apple trees, one crab apple and a pear. Brambles around the borders. In his own way Silas was a stickler.' (I always enjoyed the way Geoff referred to his father by his Christian name. I can't ever remember calling my father Stanley.)

'Then there was the poultry. We kept Khaki hens because they laid more eggs than any other breed. There was a big cage of chickens for their eggs and their meat. Turkeys, bred up for sale at Christmas. Geese, very fashionable in those days, and Aylesbury ducks as fat as we could make them – for sale at Christmas – a big penful, better not get in the middle of them! You had to work at it.' Geoff laughed out loud. 'Silas was a hard man to keep up with. He built a low-level greenhouse for roses and tomatoes. Roses for Mam. She loved roses, especially pinks.'

Every time I read these lists which embrace so many aspects of that small village, I marvel at the determination, the guts and the skills to turn a hard, virtually intransigent wasteland into such a civilised, deep-reaching place.

I thought that Wigton was unbeatable but in Fletchertown, on those black nights when we fitted in the last game before I caught the late bus back to Wigton, there was such a vibrant feeling of being alive, with Geoff, Brian and sometimes Peter and Colin, hunting after other families – with no ill intent, just play, just play, bringing on that unmistakable feeling of the acutely exciting present as our chasing games in the twilight drummed the roof of the empty caves and tunnels below, once crammed with coal, black gold.

* * *

Another World

After 1945 there was a drift abroad. As if the war had worn out affection and loyalty for the place in which so many had struggled. The glamorous and tempting brochures and reports from the Empire came down like manna. There would be sun. There could be equal opportunity. There would be a better life.

In Wigton it was release for many. The Hewers went to Cartmel on the West Coast of the USA; the Postlethwaite family went to New York. The young Muirhead boys set off for Canada, the Moffatts for Tasmania, the Studholmes and the Wallaces for Australia. The Robsons and the Sinclairs to New Zealand. My father's youngest brother went to Australia and but for his devotion to my mother, and her devotion to Wigton, he would have followed. And so it grew, the route of the Ten Pound Poms, the great escape to lands that promised hospitality and opportunity which an exhausted Britain could no longer deliver.

And from Fletchertown, Peggy Littlefair, the captain of the women's cricket team, and her daughter, Alwyn, who had been in the same class at school as me and who keeps in touch, and Ursula Nixon from Silloth who found poetry and contentment with new friends in Australia, away from the prejudices of the north . . . on it went, the great escape, the lure of change, the resolution to make a new life in a new place on their own terms. All sailed away . . . to what generally proved to be a tough life, far from the brochures.

Chapter Ten

Along with Alan, Ulick and Robert, we formed a casual Oxford club and tried to earn our salt by taking up, rather formally, ideas that were in the wind. For instance: when will schools and universities cease to be based on memory tests? When will you be allowed to take textbooks into the exams, flip to the facts, draw your conclusions to the question and write an original essay, an attempt to think it through for yourself? Why spend such time and energy in learning by heart what is there at the turn of a page? And learning by heart is so soon wiped out. What is the point these days in merely regurgitating swotting?

Alan was often on his best sermonising form. 'There's a satisfaction in learning by heart,' he conceded, 'but the time it takes and its predominance is no longer necessary. When we look back at the surgical operational techniques of the Middle Ages, we find most of them barbarous compared with what we can do now. Is what we do now in teaching any longer fit for purpose? The unimaginable increase in information means that such heavy lifting stretches memory too much and ties it up when it could spend its resources being freer, more enjoyable, more creative. Is it a skill that is useful for an increasing number of tasks? Is it even reliable long term? How much of the memory bank you build up at school in adolescence or even at university remains in useful recall? Or does it just clutter up the brain like the junk in space?'

The best of university, we concluded, was what you learned to pick up for yourself in three gift-wrapped years. It isn't surprising that much of what we take back from university, we agreed, is often not on the curriculum: friends, of course, but also unexpected opportunities. We were unanimous – and went to the pub. 'I think we've concluded that Oxford is a waste of time,' said Alan with some satisfaction. Our club soon lost its vim. It lapsed because it was formal and pretentious: random chat was richer.

I was lucky with the tutors who devoted their time to the likes of us raw recruits, and something of their influence remains – more a way of thinking than a stash of details, a method of organising thought, a sense of perspective. The greatest learning was probably self-taught outside the College walls. Acting, writing, rugby, rowing, film-making, squash, wide reading, public speaking, journalism, these and other off-campus pursuits were to develop talents that began as a private passion and would sometimes mature into a profession.

* * *

In the week after I came back to Oxford from Wigton, I walked along Walton Street. It was part of the drifting I enjoyed, especially in the evening. The Oxford University Press was in that street and a cinema, the Scala.

There was this poster. It was Sarah. Sarah in a big close-up. Sarah looking upset. Sarah through and through. I went in. The second shock was that the film was in Swedish with English subtitles, the first I'd ever seen – or read. It seized my imagination like no other I had ever seen save for *Snow White and the Seven Dwarfs* when I was seven . . .

In Wigton I went to Saturday matinées as regularly as to Sunday Eucharist. When we got to the pub, there were two complimentary tickets as payment for displaying a poster of the three films on that week. I only rarely failed to make use of them with William or Eric. There are still films from the forties and early fifties that I remember vividly. Cowboy movies. Gangsters. Musicals. Comedies. Wars. Adventures. Epics. And only very rarely was I not swept up in them, most of all in the male leading characters whose mannerisms I would ape for a day or so and whose reputations would always lure me to their next appearance. This intoxication began with *Snow White and the Seven Dwarfs*, which I managed, at the age of seven, to see three times over one weekend. Stars included Alan Ladd, Edward G. Robinson, John Wayne, Errol Flynn . . . What strikes me now is that these glamorous Hollywood actors had often been hired from the streets and carried the tang of real life with them, however extravagantly they were made up and made over. There was a basic connection between the mass population and the on-screen characters.

I was film hardened. But nothing had prepared me for seeing Ingmar Bergman in Oxford. *Port of Call*, an early work of Bergman's, was the film postered at the Scala. It was the first of his films I saw and by his standards plain and simple. Bergman was probably the most revelatory subject I got from Oxford. I was mesmerised.

It is still difficult to explain to myself why I was and am still so locked into Bergman, and to a slightly lesser degree to the films of other European directors that I saw at Oxford in that time. Truffaut, Renoir, Chabrol, De Sica, Visconti, Rossellini, Fellini . . . Perhaps there's a clue in the way that from the beginning I talked about these films – it was 'a Bergman film', 'a Renoir', 'a Fellini' where in Wigton, films had been plugged by the leading actors – John Wayne, Kirk Douglas, Rita Hayworth. Directors were invisible. Now I looked out for the guiding talent of the director. For me, directors were the new stars and they brought a different quality to the way I saw the films. It was more like reading D.H. Lawrence, or *L'Étranger*, or Joyce or *Buddenbrooks*. It had a relentless intensity. Many of us fell under Bergman's spell.

There was something in his films that for all the characters and incidents had a clear individual vision, even a philosophy, underlying it. I went on to be immersed in the work of the man behind the screen, at all times, the puppet master, the playmaker, to hear and see his vision threading throughout, speaking with one voice underlying all the others. Bergman's grip and style were reinforced by the cast of actors he worked with in the theatre. They took that group integrity with them into films. Maybe being in a foreign language gave it for me an intellectual glamour – no more than that? – but there *was* more than that and a whole generation of us felt it and fell for it and saw films as Cinema and the Pictures as a cultural force, a new treasure, and not only European but Japanese – Kurosawa – and Indian – Satyajit Ray – and Mexican – Buñuel.

I think that something different happened. The brain sought out and found new sensations. When I came out of *Port of Call*, and with increasing conviction in those three years at university, I felt it. I watched Bergman's films, often twice, especially when I began reviewing them. It was as if I were determined to hold on to them, through *Summer Interlude*, *Summer with Monika*, *Sawdust and Tinsel*, *Smiles of a Summer Night*, *Wild Strawberries*, *The Virgin Spring* ... and, most embracingly, *The Seventh Seal* on which I was to write a short book for the BFI Film Classics series. Here the mediaeval world reached us in the most modern medium.

I know, though, that I will always find it impossible to explain accurately why the experience I went through with Bergman's films, and later some of those of his European contemporaries, added a new dimension to a brilliant alchemy of this new art. It was new to us then and yet it carried all the history of old character and storytelling ways.

Bergman's films continue to be the marker against which for me all films are judged. He put everything into them – from what I can gather his films spent his life. The work became the man and what was left over seems to have been a trail of sexual confusion. Like many other artists, he was driven to put the best of himself into his work, the lees were left for life. Perhaps, as has been said, you cannot have perfection in the life and in the work.

When I came to London, it was a relief to find that the Academy Cinema in Oxford Street showed Bergman films. Woody Allen, besotted with Bergman, made a film attempting to replicate him. He got everything right except the core of it, that which made Bergman intellectually and emotionally authentic. Allen's take was hollow.

Bergman's later, more nakedly psychological films use long close-ups ('There is nothing more dramatic than the face,' he once said) which print themselves on your mind as he encourages his leading actresses especially to give their own most profound feelings to the camera. I had never seen anything like it.

* * *

In an animated way, I talked about this with Michael Wolfers in his rooms on another late night when yet again I had made use of the Trespasser's Window.

He decided that I should be a film critic and fixed it for *Cherwell*, the flourishing undergraduate weekly. Michael had university connections that I knew nothing about. There was an opportunity, another fluke of luck to my advantage in a life that has been studded with such strokes. Within two or three weeks I was being interviewed by Michael Billington, an undergraduate editor of the arts pages in *Cherwell*, and told that a gap had opened up in the film critic slot and would I do it for a short stint as a try-out? I did. And largely thanks to the editing of Michael Billington, my reviews were printed. I got the job. I was swept into the university film business with the cautious blessing of the editor who would go on to edit the *Manchester Guardian*.

It set off a modest chain reaction. My name in *Cherwell* increased the nodding quotient in the quad. Fame! Comments! A nod in the quad! All because of Michael's window of opportunity. I reviewed many of Bergman's films in *Cherwell*.

And new stars came in this Swedish constellation to outshine the Anglo-Americans: Max von Sydow, Gunnar Björnstrand, Bibi Andersson and others who had worked with Bergman in the theatre. A new planet had swum into my ken. 'Foreign' films keyed some of us into another way of seeing and thinking.

For some time I had secretly entertained an ambition to be a writer. The confidence of Oxford was sympathetic to such an ambition. The fearful lid that had capped the impulse at school was off. I wrote two short stories in that first term, but it was the Bergman bug which had seized me. He was traditional; he was new; he was radical; he was always based in carefully observed life. My secret ambition now was to be a writer and a film director. I had never had such a clear objective. It seemed further away than Pluto.

* * *

Kipling said that you should always read aloud anything you write. At Oxford I had read aloud a lengthy essay three times a fortnight to tutors whose ear for style was as acute as their mind for facts. It was a time of writing gracefully and two of my tutors by hints and encouragement tried to pass it on.

At school Mr Blacker had made us read aloud from the poems, plays and essays in our 'set' books. And the grooming on *Cherwell* by eager and more practised contemporaries commanded its own disciplines on space and clarity.

Most embarrassing but perhaps most influential of all, I had at school begun to write poetry. Prompted by an appeal from the school magazine, there are poems, some of which I can still remember and hardly bear.

When I wrote them I had not absorbed the example and the teaching of Wordsworth – the plain speaking, the common tongue allied with the flexibility to access the grandest reaches of magnificent and magisterial poetic glory. His works radicalised the idea of great poetry and did so through a unique dedication to the language of ordinary people infused with a passion for the power of nature to teach and shape the mind. And, significantly for me, the place he chose for the laboratory of the mind was the Lake District. His part of the world was one I could and did bike to see and be part of. It was thrilling to walk where he had walked, to hear his lines in the places that had inspired them, to be an apprentice.

However, that took time to percolate through the classroom on to the page. Meanwhile, for the school magazine I was a very long way from Wordsworth and I just let rip! Here goes – for instance, aged fourteen, when religion mattered every bit as much as nature. Deep breath:

> Time is the gift of man to God,
> For God's eternity knows no time
> But man is bounded by it.
> The timeless of God is, then true paradise
> For there, free from Time's care,
> Man can know himself, and, through time,
> Know God . . .

A long, long way from:

> She dwelt among the untrodden ways
> Beside the springs of Dove,
> A Maid whom there were none to praise
> And very few to love.

Another World

Or the shortest but most profound philosophical musings in the language, beginning:

> One impulse from a vernal wood
> May teach you more of man,
> Of moral evil and of good,
> Than all the sages can.

You start somewhere.

* * *

That first short story happened on an afternoon in Oxford when there must have been a gap in my schedule. I remember starting it, out of nowhere, finishing it about four hours later, rather bemused at seeing the three filled pages.

It was set in Greenwood, the Georgian mansion a couple of miles from Wigton to which my mother biked twice a week to clean. In the school holidays she put me on the pillion of her heavy bike and pedalled there, instructing me to stick out my legs as high as possible when we passed certain farms with hungry guard dogs baying and rushing to the gate. I loved Greenwood.

I have previously written about this place, especially its owner, Mrs Cavaghan, widowed at the start of the war, and her two children, Annette and George, who were such memorable playmates. I showed the story to no one. I made no copies and I have lost it.

It did, however, send out a signal. A signal to whom? Myself. I could do it! Whatever the outcome, I could and I would write from then on, if only to rediscover that happy daze. It soon became clearer than that. As soon as I left university I started a routine of writing which over the last sixty years I have pursued. It is the doing of it, of letting a pen draw out thoughts and actions, establish, in some lucky cases, an indivisible bond. Silence speaks out of silence to silence. Words alone evoke words which, if the writer is good enough or lucky enough, and the reader receptive, act like a transplant. It is strong magic. And for me it makes life work. Like all other writers, it makes sense at the time and satisfies an impulse as convincing as it is fugitive.

I would like to think that the work, the writing I have done since Oxford, was seeded in that first afternoon in Wadham. In the sense of finding a unique satisfaction in just starting and finding a story that for me rang true. For the most part what I wrote after university had only one drive, which was to write, rewrite and write unceasingly – from the start with unfinished novels, and then settling to draw on the underdescribed richness of 'ordinary life', often picking out stories from Wigton. Finally in *For Want of a Nail* at the third draft I thought it clicked. It was a proper novel, I thought, and so did the agent Richard Simon, to whom I'd been recommended by a poet in the BBC. He found a publisher. Now it was work through the day and writing at night. It took over. I had stumbled into a vocation and a subject.

* * *

When I started *The South Bank Show* in 1977 I wrote to Ingmar Bergman. A previous request had been briefly, politely enough, declined. I told him that there was going to be a new arts series, no limits on subject matter and, I suppose, I pestered him . . . Finally he agreed to a meeting in Munich – it was a tough lunch. The meeting was more like an audition for me. For him it was an opportunity to speak English and assess whether it would serve. He agreed to do the film.

For filming in the Munich studios we were allocated a small, plain, dull room. He came in, looked around, half opened the door which would be behind him in the interview, courteously ushered the key camera a couple of yards to his left, and it was a film set. He coughed loudly, theatrically. We began.

The regret I still have is that this was very early on in my career – my first year as an interviewer and editor and I had not developed the confidence, as I did later with David Lean and Laurence Olivier and others, to let it run into two programmes. Still, one was fulfilment enough. All of us glowed as we got on the plane back to London. We had Ingmar Bergman on the programme! And in the archives still today at Leeds University are the hours of unused footage from that interview which may yet find a space in some documentary.

I think his genius came from something like a religious passion. He came from a severe Lutheran background which he both nursed and attacked. His conviction was driven by faith. In that first interview he said: 'You put a chair on a stage. You say it is a throne. You sit on it. You say I am a king. If you do it well – everyone believes you.' He made his actors believe they were the characters he had written. Their talents were their own. But their conversion on screen was, I think, fashioned by a believer. I have also thought that he hypnotised them.

I phoned him, once, years later. It was embarrassing. It was about three o'clock in the morning. I was living in a cottage in North Cumbria – a landscape in its grandeur, its comparative emptiness, its dramatic possibilities and its loneliness very like parts of Sweden. I had drunk far too much in the pub and walked back the mile or so uphill to the cottage, one of seven dwellings in a hamlet on the fell. On the way I was seized with a brilliant idea for a Bergman film. I rehearsed it as I swayed up and up to the cottage.

There, in front of a dead fire, my wife and children in bed asleep, I called Mr Bergman and got his answerphone. I reeled off the outline of the masterpiece he was destined to turn into a film: the lifelong dispute between two religious hill farmers, brothers, who had married twins.

The following morning I woke up with a chronic hangover and a painful sense of my stupidity.

There was a perfect response on the answerphone.

'Thank you.'

Chapter Eleven

Oxford relishes its mediaevalism – the colleges, the history, the gowns, the whole weaving of the place over nigh on nine hundred years. It is the major factor in defining its unique character. But it is the Grace, in Latin, before dinner which most firmly clings to and celebrates its origins.

It is a two-hand drama. The Warden of the College and a scholar.

Scholars wear long black gowns on a par with those worn by the tutors, the dons. Non-scholars – the majority – wear short gowns, jacket size, known as 'bum-freezers'.

A senior scholar selects the speakers, turn by turn. In my case, the chief scholar was from one of the mighty northern grammar schools, very confident. He was trying to turn himself into an upper-middle-class dandy. He was clever, sharp and sure of his newly acquired accent. When it came to my turn – in the second year – I was given a pep talk by this chief scholar, delivered at such speed that it confused my painstakingly rehearsed version.

I stood at one end of the High Table peopled by dons and occasional honoured guests. Far away at the other end stood the Warden – in this case Sir Maurice Bowra. There was the problem of his deafness, but all you could do was to forge on. He used a hearing aid which he declared to be 'very good for knives and forks'. The Grace had to be learned by heart. There was always the feeling that out there among the standing ranks of the black-gowned men there would be those quite pleased to note mistakes. It was as much a trial of nerves as memory.

I was all but frozen in apprehension. It was like those times when I was younger and felt my mind slip out of my body. How could I get it back? However often I had rehearsed it, suddenly the words failed me. A kickstart to the early, rather simple exchanges got me going but it was neck and neck and running dry. Someone else out there was doing the talking. Whoever the 'I' was stood his ground robotically and somewhere the words came out, toneless, fragile, desperate – not too heavy a description. There was no safety net. There was no stopping and in my head there seemed no guarantee that I could remember the words, let alone remember them in the right order. Confidence all but collapsed and I clung on to the wreckage for fear of letting go. Exaggerated?

No.

When the Warden banged the long table with his gavel, there was silence, and I had to fill it. Latin had always been my weakest subject! The English translation is here to help the reader. The dining room congregation was expected to follow the Latin.

I took a deep breath and began.

Scholar: Benedictus Deus in donis suis
   (Blessed be God in his gifts)
Warden: Et sanctus in omnibus operibus suis
   (And holy in all his works)
Scholar: Adjutorium nostrum in nomine Domini
   (Our aid in the name of the Lord)

Another World

Warden: Qui fecit coelum et terram
(Who made Heaven and Earth)
Scholar: Sit nomen Dei benedictum
(Let God's name be blessed)
Warden: Ex hoc usque in saecula saeculorum
(From now and for ever more)
Scholar: Domine salvam fac Elizabetham Reginam
(God save Queen Elizabeth)
Warden: Et exaudi nos cum invocamus Te
(And hear us when we call upon Thee)
Scholar: Domine Deus, vita et resurrectio credentium, qui semper es laudandus, tum in viventibus, tum in defunctis, agimus Tibi gratias pro Nicolao Wadhamo Armigero et pro Dorothea uxore ejus, fundatoribus nostris defunctis aliisque benefactoribus, quorum beneficiis hic ad pietatem et ad studia literarum alimur, rogantes ut nos, his Tuis donis recte utentes, una cum illis ad resurrectionis gloriam perducamur, per Jesum Christum Dominum nostrum.
(Lord God, the resurrection and the life of all them that believe, who are always to be praised both in the living and the dead, we give Thee thanks for Nicholas Wadham, Knight, and for Dorothy his wife, our late founders, and all other our Benefactors by whose benefits we are here maintained in godliness and the study of letters and beseech Thee that, using Thy gifts rightly, we may be led along with them to the glory of the resurrection, through Jesus Christ our Lord.)
Amen.
(So be it).

Whatever faith or none, we stood silently to the end obeying the tradition of centuries. My legs only just functioned with enough strength for me to sit down. The low encouraging murmur of carefully gathered friends managed to quell the shaking. 'Not all bad,' said someone.

Chapter Twelve

'You *have* to have a party!'

Michael was gleeful. His wide smile widened further. He saw one of the problems immediately. Gerald, who donned pyjamas at ten, would not be happy.

'We could hold it here.' He looked around. 'I'll tidy it up. We *must* throw a party for her.'

I had called in on a Saturday morning to tap Michael's brains. He was in a social circuit which rolled around ceaselessly. He was also by far the most helpful person Oxford had put my way. Sarah's train would arrive just after three. I would arrive half an hour before then.

'I'll bring the wine,' I said.

'Make it very cheap.' Michael was in earnest. 'We'll get it in the College bar. They take returns.' He was emphatic. 'None of us knows about quality and all they want is to talk to each other. And about each other, usually.'

'The problem is . . .' I began.

'You don't know any girls!' Michael was even more gleeful.

'I can't expect her to be the only girl in the room.'

'I'll fix that.' He paused, but only for a moment. 'Saturday . . . Saturday . . . I've a couple of things at sixish . . . I could skip Trinity, a bit too grand for me in any case, it's one of the colleges that make me feel not so much a fly on the wall as a grub in the shrubbery ... there's Pembroke, that's always fun. I have friends there ...'

'You have friends everywhere.'

'There are more than forty men I knew before I came here and the numbers just grow and grow!' He giggled. 'They can't *all* want their names in *Cherwell*. There must be *some*thing else involved.' Then suddenly he exclaimed, '*Cherwell*! That's what we'll have. A *Cherwell* party. Some of them will bring a bottle. Crisps will be quite enough to eat. *Cherwell*! Yes. Weeks ahead of the big end-of-term Christmas parties – just a little touch of *Cherwell* in the evening! *And* of course' – there was an almost coquettish smile – 'they will produce the female of the species!'

'Done!'

'Tomorrow?'

'One day's notice can be construed as rather stylish,' he said. 'I have some postcards of paintings in the Royal Academy. Quite smart.' He was in full flood. 'I'll use them as invitations. I can play postman while you wait at the station. How exciting!'

There was still the matter of getting through the first evening.

The initial disappointment was the small bed and breakfast in a house in a street next to the College. I had booked a single room.

'No gentlemen allowed in the ladies' rooms at any time. If you would like a cup of tea together there is the small parlour next to the dining room. Gentlemen must be out by nine o'clock. Ladies are expected to sign in no later than half past ten unless special permission has been requested in advance. Breakfast half past seven to nine.'

Mrs Rogers's tone was as iron grey as her cropped hair.

'Sign here,' she commanded Sarah, who did as she was bid.

'Which college?'

'Wadham.'

'Several of your young gentlemen choose us.' She smiled in self-congratulation.

'What's the room like?'

'Very clean.' Sarah smiled. 'The bed is small even for a single person.' She laughed – we were back on the street now. 'And it's very cold.'

'We could have a walk or a drink.'

'Both.'

* * *

'It's a cosy little pub, isn't it?' Sarah was making an effort to enjoy Everything.

'Oxford's full of them. Worse than Wigton.'

She looked around at the indisputably 'upper' clientele. 'It's pleasant,' she said. 'I'll give it that.'

'Where would you like to go next?'

'You're in charge. But I've seen enough buildings.'

'Which did you like best?'

'I knew you'd say that! You won't stop . . .' She shook her head. 'All of them . . . I'm not that interested in buildings . . . that place where they were martyred, that was good.'

'You took a bit of convincing about the Lake District at first,' I said.

'I did . . . Maybe Oxford would grow on me if I came often enough. It doesn't seem very real at the moment. But it's different. I can see why people take to it. People like you . . .' She paused. 'People it means something to. I could tell you thought it was great from the moment we set off on your tour.'

'It was just a walk.'

'It was a tour. You like to point things out . . . I suppose it would be different if I lived here. It's all a bit grand. So are the students.'

'Why don't you come and live here? There are banks in Oxford.'

'We've been through that.' But she smiled, looked wonderfully warm, easily the most attractive person in the bar.

'What's wrong with going through it again?'

'I haven't got used to the first time yet! You always rush things. I'm a stranger here. This visit will do for now. My round.'

She went to the bar and I watched her as closely as if I were studying someone rare and valuable, unlike any other and fully known only to me. Her entry into this alien world had skittled all other assumptions: that would do. It was Sarah I wanted to live with me.

While she queued for the drinks, I looked around the tweedy, the jolly good-mannered, almost loud clients, mostly men; everywhere you went it was mostly men, and Sarah's arrival had made that even more obvious. Long black hair, slim, a slightly weathered complexion, slyly glanced at by the clientele.

'What would you like to do?'

Take her to my room in Wadham. Hope that luck was on my side and Gerald had nipped off to see his parents. Put on the fire, open a bottle of wine, and be fully together, a cosy way of saying make love, another cosy way of stating the obvious. But Gerald had given no hint that he would disappear. Had he been set on that track there would have been a neat, clear note on the mantelpiece which I would surely have caught earlier on.

'We could always go to the pictures.'

'We go to the pictures in Wigton.'

'But this film is fantastic . . .'

'And you want to see it again?'

I outlined the plot of *The Virgin Spring*. The rape of an innocent young woman, the revenge on the rapists including the killing of a child, the miracle at the end, the Virgin Spring. 'It's in Swedish,' I finished. 'But the subtitles are great. I think they make it better in a way.'

For a moment her look froze as if she were being confronted with a freak. She spoke slowly.

'You *have* to be joking. In *Swedish*?'

I drew a deep breath. But then she began to laugh, a full-throated unaffected laugh, infectious. 'I thought you came here to write essays.'

'We do, but there's time over.'

'I see.' She was mockingly solemn. 'What else?'

'Well. Some do a lot of sport, others debate in the Union, others act in plays or set up committees, or sing in choirs or drink too much or whatever takes their fancy.'

'Or their money.'

'As far as it stretches, yes. Some of them are rich.'

'And what do not rich people like you do when you should be writing essays?'

'All sorts. I've started to write about the pictures, about films, for the university newspaper.'

'What use is that?'

'You never know.'

'You mean you want to be a reporter? You could have done that by getting a start in Carlisle with the *Cumberland News*.'

'That isn't the point.'

Sarah was enjoying herself. She looked stunning.

'You can't do essays all the time.' It was the only defence I had.

She paused. And nodded. And then laughed again. 'What a fiddle!'

'No it isn't. You'll meet some people who write for *Cherwell* tomorrow night at the party.'

'Whose party?'

'Ours!'

She shook her head very slowly. 'You're having me on.'

'And I thought on Monday we could go to the theatre.'

'Hold on! A party, a theatre – anything else?'

'I know it's a bit cold but I thought we might get a boat and row on the river in the afternoon. Or we could go for a walk in the parks. You'd like them.'

'You've got it all planned.'

'. . . Most of it.'

'You always do.' She shook her head.

'Not always. You know that. Not always.'

'Is there a pub with music?'

'Not that I know . . . there's a dance hall, a bit like the County in Carlisle.'

Sarah was now fully enjoying herself.

'So we come to Oxford to go to the County in Carlisle.'

'Or we could still go to *The Virgin Spring*.'

Another World

'Where are your friends? Alan, Ulick, isn't it? Robert?'

'If they're not at a party, I'd put my money on the bar of the Wadham pub.'

'Let's go there.'

She lifted the glass of red wine.

'Cheers!' she said. 'Drink up. Remember I have to be back in the witch's castle by half past ten on the dot or the door will be barred and padlocked!'

We went to the pub. Ulick and Robert were there. They were pleased to see us. They liked Sarah, they told me later; and she liked them, as she told me later. It was a Friday night of friendship, warm noise and, for Sarah, uncomplicated satisfying congeniality.

'It is a bit like Wigton after all,' she said, as we walked back. I kept a lookout for a dark and twisting alley or a deeply set doorway in Holywell Street, but no luck. Sarah wouldn't have been up for it anyway. Oxford had brought out her best behaviour.

Chapter Thirteen

Michael had lit candles.

'Dress to impress,' he said. 'The room, that is. Parties should bring out the worst in us.' His wide smile in the candlelight gave him a wicked look. 'There's red and white, and orange juice if you must.'

He was the spirit of the event. His books had been rearranged on the shelves in orderly library rows. Three abstract paintings I'd barely noticed before now hung in prominent splendour saying, 'Would you like to ask me what I am?' He was still of course wearing his dark suit and a tie. It was a pleasure to be in the company of someone taking such pleasure in the company of others. Names were flung around proudly, introductions made with a smile or a giggle and after the original burn of self-consciousness, Sarah laughed along. When he teased her, she warned, 'Michael, if you say that once more . . .' She knew a friend when she saw one.

Most of the guests had brought a bottle which Michael had anticipated and therefore directed me to be discreet with my contribution from the College cellar, saying, 'Put theirs at the front; ours is returnable. We'll put them on the reserve table.' Crisps were freely strewn about in saucers and dishes. Music was requested by one of the more callow guests but instantly banned by Michael. 'Why have music when we have some of the best gossips in Oxford? Music ruins conversation.' The only don who had come along was Dr Keeley with his dog.

At one stage I reverted to type and took bottles around to feed empty glasses, but Michael wouldn't have it. 'Sarah, tell him "No"!' he said firmly. And to me, 'Stick by her. She's shy and she's a lamb in a field of these terrible Oxford wolves. Your job is to look after her.' There was no humour in his voice. There was even severity. 'They're very pleasant,' she whispered, 'but I don't know what to say. It's the way they talk about just everything. They never stop!'

It was the first such party I had been to. A couple of the dons had dispensed dry sherry for an hour or so near the beginning of term. There were Warden Bowra's bombastic soirées, the rugby club could dissipate into drinks in the cellar bar after a home game, but not a party! I had spotted them on a Saturday evening, windows open to let the cool air in and the exclusive noise drift out. They had not been on my circuit. There were always the pubs, but they did not classify.

So this was the Real Thing. Robert, Ulick and Alan were there which was a relief. Sarah felt they were some kind of guard. I could see her relax, watched as she got involved in those rather loud snatches of talk in the crowded room and soon, when I looked across the room to find her, she was oblivious of me, talking to a sports jacket and brown corduroys, which was the best thing that could have happened. It turned out they were talking about farming. Her questioner was to inherit an estate in the Highlands.

What else was the talk? At this distance group talk on cheap drink is not easy to recall with much accuracy, but one thing is certain: the talk would have been largely about themselves and those like them and their doings interspersed with a few headlines from the papers.

Many of them were aiming for a career in journalism and a few of them got there. France's problem with Algeria was shuttled around as several of them had been to France in the previous summer. As had I. From the open windows in the school where I worked in the Bois de Vincennes, I had listened to and been excited by the gunfire in the woods at night.

Sentences drifted increasingly loudly across the overpacked room. Would Pasternak get the Nobel Prize and if he got it, would he be allowed to accept it? Was Duke Ellington the best jazzman in the business? Was jazz better than classical? Speculation on the atomic bomb – but soon back to Them. To *Us*, I suppose. Michael Billington's most recent column: 'Could Oxford be taken seriously when it was so monstrously masculine?' 'Bergman's new film: is he repeating himself?' and the lesser and lesser chat: 'We're going skiing in the New Year . . . we are . . . I am . . . are you?' . . . just bumping into people and making the best of the accidental encounter. Grazing was more important than heavy discussion.

Quotations from Bowra were common. One phrase came from Michael Wolfers' latest assembly when someone had complained that the garden party he was offering would be hobbled by so many who were strangers to each other: 'At a party never speak to anyone you know,' he said, 'that's cheating.' I rather expected – and hoped – he would suddenly come into the room and turn it into one of those quotable parties with Evelyn Waugh memorialising them. And how could we enjoy Waugh so much when he had supported Franco? But how could we not? And how could you listen to Wagner when he was antisemitic? They both had genius, didn't that beat prejudice? Back to who was leading which pack and back to Michael with his effortless omnivorous knowledge of the doings of his contemporaries.

'So,' said Michael, as he, Alan, myself and Sarah tidied up after the last guest had gone, 'I'd give it alpha-beta, or maybe beta-alpha. We can't give it a straight alpha because we did not attract the Outstanding Person or Persons who make a column sing. But still, it had its own bounce. And now,' he said, 'I shall have my first drink of the evening. And you see! Your College bottles still stand, untouched, unopened. I'll take them back tomorrow morning for a full rebate when I return the glasses.'

He waved us goodnight and thanked Sarah for giving him the opportunity to throw a party he had meant to throw for months. 'I'll have coffee on the boil tomorrow morning,' he said. 'It's my form of Sunday worship.'

We strolled back to her hotel; the street was barely habited.

'Well?'

'I knew you'd ask that.' Sarah looked directly at me, a street light full on her face. She was uncertain. We slowed down.

'They're very polite,' she said. 'All of them. Ulick and Robert and Alan of course, and Michael – he's so kind, isn't he? He seemed so happy and yet at the same time I felt sorry for him. I don't know why. But they were, all of them, so good-mannered.'

'You looked comfortable.'

Sarah hesitated.

'I wouldn't say I was. I didn't want to let you down. I was sticking it out.'

'Oh! That's terrible.'

'It isn't terrible. It's the way it is . . . Did you notice the clothes that the girls were wearing? Of course you didn't. Well, all of them wore what I would call flowery dresses, rather flowing, very classy I thought. Mine looked too tight-fitting.'

'You looked better than any of them.'

'I looked out of place. This thin red belt around my waist is wrong. And their hairstyles were so different from mine. They were very pleasant but I felt out of it . . .'

'I didn't notice that.'

'You wouldn't.' She smiled. 'You never notice what I'm wearing. But I still enjoyed it. I really did. And there were some nice people there, even though I felt I was talking like a bumpkin. It's just . . . Here we are.'

'That's such a shame.'

'I honestly enjoyed it. It's just that I didn't expect it to be so different.'

I watched her go in and paused awhile as if waiting for a miracle: when the door would reopen, Mrs Witch would be all smiles and she would point the way to the stairs.

When we met the next morning Sarah was carrying a parcel.

'I got this as a present for Michael yesterday. It would have been showing off to give it to him last night, so I hid it under my coat.'

She was dressed more casually.

The quad was Sunday suited.

The chapel bell rang on cue.

Michael was waiting.

'Perfect!' He looked proudly at the arrangement on the small table. 'This is how you make what looks like expensive coffee and, for some, tastes like expensive coffee, but it's all sleight of hand. You take a tin of common Nescafé, spoon it carefully into the three cups, then you take the just-off-the-boil water and hold the kettle high and engineer a sort of cascade effect to make it frothy. Milk to taste, smarter not. Sugar of course compulsory to take the edge off the terrible tang of the coffee. There we are . . . Cheers!'

Sarah handed over the present, or rather she thrust it at Michael, blushing. 'This is for you. For your party. Thank you.'

'Oh! Thank you! May I?' He opened it. Sarah had bought a silk scarf in deep red and blue. Michael held it as if it were a treasure from Tutankhamen's tomb. 'It's beautiful!' He flung it around his neck. There was without question a suggestion of tears. I thought of the boy whose parents had been killed in Germany and whose transplantation to England had been so austere. Few presents there. 'It's really beautiful, and so kind,' he said. He paused, and then he collected himself. 'I shall be the talk of Broad Street!' He fiddled with the scarf a little, tied it loosely, stroked it; then he beamed . . .

The highlight of the Sunday was the open-air production of *A Midsummer Night's Dream* in Worcester College. Postponed twice since summer, a warm burst of weather provided an opportunity to remount what was to be hailed as a landmark production. Worcester College contained notable gardens and a small lake, which was perfect for their production.

Another World

It began at three o'clock. There was a blanket on every seat. Incidental music was sung by the Christ Church choir. The woods and the lake were cunningly lit by oil lamps and candles. Neither Sarah nor I had seen anything like it. You would have thought she had turned to stone. She sat, swaddled in the tartan blanket, picking up every crumb.

'That,' she said later in the inevitable pub to warm us up, 'was the best thing I've ever seen.'

Whatever reservations and hesitations had been growing about her Oxford Experience, *A Midsummer Night's Dream* had wiped them away.

We went to that pub, knowing it would be cosy, crowded, for pie and chips, but most importantly, for Cliff, who was the scout on Staircase Two. He was engaged in a fierce inter-pub battle of shove ha'penny. When the competition was over he invited me to 'have a go' (useless) and then Sarah ('got the hang of it quite quickly').

Later we talked about the play.

'I liked it when he was turned into a donkey,' she said.

'We did it at school – I was the one who turned into a donkey. Bottom the Weaver.'

'I wish I'd seen that. I really wish I'd seen you as a donkey! And called Bottom! I'll remember that.'

A rushed essay on Monday morning when Sarah insisted that she wanted to wander around on her own, lunch at George's in the market, according to Michael the best and cheapest meal in Oxford, and then at snail's progress to the station, the waving goodbye, the feeling empty.

She had posted me a letter – in Oxford – which I got the next day. It was a loving letter.

Life was good.

Chapter Fourteen

There was a documentary on BBC television about life in Oxford. I saw it a few months before I went up. Called *The Glittering Coffin*, it was written and presented by a young undergraduate called Dennis Potter. After university he would go on to become the defining playwright of a new television age rich in original drama. He became a Voice in the land.

In the documentary, there was a rather shy, good-looking and handsomely dressed undergraduate, the usual sports jacket and cavalry twills. Expensive, upper class glowing off him.

Potter asked him, 'Do you resent the arrival of the working class here at Oxford?' To his credit, I thought then and still do, the young man spoke rather quietly but firmly, 'Yes, I do rather.'

Potter had netted his catch. Good-mannered old-fashioned snobbery, in its delivery as inoffensive as snobbery could be. When I recalled the encounter, I saw how far it was from Ulick or Robert and realised that there was no room for generalisations, and yet Potter saw it as a blanket class judgement. He was wrong. Given the similarity of our backgrounds, Potter's and mine, it was a lesson. Generalisations here were fruitless.

We made them all the time. Oxford after the Second World War became increasingly available to a wider cross-section of our society. But it was a slow burn and we were expected to conform. To become like Them. Still heavily tilted towards the privileged. This was only the beginning of a gradual redistribution. At Oxford, the artisan and working class were a small clan in my time but rather effectively persuasive. The right wing, who were rich, landed and influential before Oxford, were destined to be rich, landed and influential afterwards. They were aware that what waited for them was one of the Establishment berths filled by people like them. Then there were those who became the Establishment professionals who would run the law or education, who would advise and often comprise the senior civil service and the government. They managed the state, although curiously, and I think unfortunately management was not on the curriculum. You were expected to imbibe it with the air you breathed. There were others sharpening careers in journalism, in literature and the theatre, poets in their favourite cafes, men whose close interests were now unleashed in their devotion to music, sport, intense scholarship – a host of tributaries trickling down the Olympian mountain of Oxford, seeking to find the conditions to kickstart a career on the back of a degree. In that sense the calm uniform exterior of the place was an illusion: the scramble for prominence was everywhere. Apart from inheritance, Oxford was next to winning the birth lottery, the best guarantee of a rewarding future you could wish for. The perfect launch pad. Or so it was thought.

And here we all were, in varying degrees of advantage, burnishing the brain for the Great Leap Forward. You could argue that the mere fact that we – men and women – were

Another World

at Oxford and would carry the Oxford label for life gave the place, for many, an ineradicable elitist shimmer. You could also argue that it produced a smug, self-serving elite.

* * *

I met Gavin Millar at an earnest debate on contemporary British films. The connection between us came about when both of us decided to walk out of the debate at the same time. After the Continental fare at the Scala, British films seemed too lightweight to discuss. It was a shallow view. We went to the nearest pub and ordered half pints of bitter. We decided to make a film.

It was not easy. The Oxford Film Society had been bankrupted by profligate spending, and the authorities were reluctant to risk financing another 'debacle' – their word. I suppose they took pity on us and I'm also sure that Gavin's script was the key factor. And the budget. We agreed to shoot it two to one – i.e. never take a scene more than twice – a very austere use of film stock – and we signed a binding document to that effect. The film was to be called *All Together Boys*. It would be about twenty minutes long. Silent, of course, and because the lead actor would have to do the donkey work, Gavin picked on me, pretending that I had something to do with its germination in the pub. It was because I was free and prepared to work hard.

I had to buy a woolly, itchy, cheap black shirt at Millets. Gavin loaned me his dark glasses.

What was it about?

Gavin never quite got round to spelling it out but the general idea was, he thought, plausible . . . The crux of the matter was that I was a rebel and wherever I went I did the opposite to everybody else. There was more to it, especially in Gavin's mind, but that's what it came down to. For instance, about a dozen of us would be sitting alongside a bar (outside drinking hours). At one point everybody stood up. Except me. At another point, everybody sat down. Except me. As I have written, Gavin was persuasive. The Oxford Actorate took it to their hearts. We were never short of extras. Another scene showed an empty meadow. Suddenly I jumped up with the girl with whom I had been hidden in the long grass. We looked around in an inquisitive way and then others – about a dozen couples – jumped up. There were even more subtle touches as the film went on. I'm afraid that after about thirty years I lost touch with it. There was only one copy made and Gavin mislaid it.

It became something of a fashionable thing to do. Richard Ingrams, who was already editing *Mesopotamia*, the progenitor of *Private Eye*, arrived with a cohort. They cheerfully did their best, raising and lowering umbrellas on a sunny day.

The end was immensely Significant. We found some old car tyres and set them alight. Then the long-suffering extras – rather reduced in number – joined hands and danced around the flames chanting Hare Krishna. There was a gasometer in the background, poignantly framed, we thought.

The film had one showing.

Gavin found an empty room in his college. He also found an American drummer who had come to Oxford to read physics and somehow acquired a drum kit. He sat at the back of the room and made a colossal din while the silent film lurched along, watched by the journalist Robert Robinson, unflinching, a London critic who was writing a feature for a London magazine on the leisure activities of this generation of Oxford students. He sat alone in the middle of the room. We crouched at the back. To his credit he mentioned us in his report, with the faintest of praise which was fair enough, and with no criticism which was a relief.

Gavin never remembered where he had mislaid it. My major legacy was a persisting chest rash from the Millets woolly shirt.

The long-term result of our effort was that Gavin and I would work together on an early BBC television arts programme at the beginning of the sixties. I, unfortunately, had been given the job of editor, which seemed okay for a few weeks until it dawned on me that my job was to give all the foreign trips on foreign artists to others. I was like those people at Bletchley in the war who pushed discs around to indicate where the planes were while the pilots took all the risks, or in our case, had all the fun. Gavin went on to make feature films, not enough, I thought. He was talented in most departments but not in hassling for commissions. His gentle, witty Midlands nature and the full-on grammar school which, like many in that part of the world and further north, was a scholarly powerhouse, had moulded modest cultural ambition.

Later, half a dozen of the Oxford colleges put together a group to tour the German universities on the Rhine with Shakespeare's last play, *The Tempest*. It was produced by Mike Sharples. Gavin, Ulick and I went along to the auditions. Ulick got the part of an aristocratic courtier; I got

Trinculo, the jester. Gavin was Stephano, the butler. Stephano and Trinculo became a tragicomic farce. A respite, a sort of onstage interval – or that seemed to be Shakespeare's intention.

I tried to persuade them to let Sarah come along, but it was no go. We would be away for four weeks. Sarah insisted that I couldn't miss such an opportunity. The calculation was that the box office takings across the tour would be a reliable subsidy. We'd hire a coach. We'd stay in university halls or in school dormitories, sometimes in private houses and once, for two days, in a monastery. The coach carried all our costumes and props – few but necessary, all skilfully compiled, we thought. We would play in city theatres and end up in Heidelberg.

The end of the war was not too far away. Curiosity was keen. The brochure of our trip looked professional, adult, and it sounded as if we knew what we were doing. The word 'Oxford', it seemed, was a pull and Shakespeare was revered in Germany. Oxford scholars talking his language were, we were told several times, a 'privilege'. The theatres were always comfortably full. First stop Marburg. And so we decanted from our coach and from then on alternatively took stylish boats down the Rhine, often accompanied by mountains topped with ornate castles. It was a fine summer. There was a glamorous tone to it despite the scars of war which were acutely felt, although we were reluctant to bring them up.

Meanwhile we performed. We were applauded and congratulated. We were well pleased with ourselves, although our director, Mike Sharples, a brooding 'method' man from Lancashire, was never done with suggestions.

Another World

Piers Plowright was the outstanding performer. He was the most striking member of the cast. Tall, broad, ridiculously handsome, the voice of a cultivated actor of the old school. Gielgud, Olivier ... a gentle, thoughtful man. He played Caliban, the monstrous, savage son of a witch who had ruled the island before the tempest brought the shipwrecked crew to find refuge there. Caliban was thought by Mike to be a pagan cannibal. He was accused of lust, even of attempted rape. He was cast radically against type in Piers.

Piers was flawlessly Christian, unafraid to profess and practise it. To watch him transfix the audience as Caliban – as he did – with a performance so far from his own character never failed to capture the rest of us on the stage. We worked as a trio – Caliban, Stephano (the butler: Gavin) and Trinculo (the fool: me). Gavin's wit carved out a droll understated character. I, frankly, bumbled around and hoped for the best. Acting stupid was one thing, making it funny was another: slapstick isn't easy. These are some of Shakespeare's more lumpen scenes with that jolliness which would have been better aimed at eight-year-olds. Over the top was the only answer. Inexplicably, people laughed. And that was our job done. 'Thank God you boys turned up,' Ulick said at the interval. 'I thought we were about to die the death.'

It revolved around Piers. We thought he would become a professional actor or a priest. He went into the BBC and became an outstanding producer on Radio Three, with bold and original documentaries, often based on music. He picked up national and international awards by the van load. On the tour he began to teach himself German, starting with the great speech in *Macbeth*, 'Morgen, morgen, und wieder morgen' – 'Tomorrow and tomorrow and tomorrow'. It became our mantra. He also played the jazz piano and . . . The danger is that he is being idolised and idealised. He would not have entertained that.

He died in 2021. By good fortune we lived close to each other for the last few decades of his life. There is so much more to say about Piers. He was brought up in the grandest part of Hampstead, Church Row, where his father was a doctor. He was married in the garden behind the house, to Poh Sim, whom he had met while in service in Malaya. She equalled him. Their mutual style and beauty was matchless.

They came down the hill from Church Row to a house in South End Green, where I would live, a less fashionable part of the suburb, near to Hampstead Heath, where Piers declared himself much happier. A bustle of a place. A railway station, the terminus for several bus routes, an enormous hospital and shops: shops the size and variety of small town shops, Wigton shops. Piers made a list of the owners of every shop – many came from the Middle East – he noted not only the names of the owners but their children, their hobbies, their ailments. We went regularly to Dominique's for one (or two) small glasses of house red and one scoop of vanilla ice cream. We knew how to live it up.

He converted to Roman Catholicism and went to a small church above Church Row. He swam in the Hampstead Ponds, sang in a local choir, did interviews in the local community centre. Three flourishing children. Have I described a perfect life? I hope so. I'm sure there were areas of darkness – where are there not? – but Piers, for me, soared above all that and perhaps Oxford had something to do with it.

His funeral was crowded. His wife, Poh Sim, was the last of those who spoke. She talked directly and quietly to the coffin as if Piers were still there. She looked around carefully. 'Hello, Piers,' she began. She paused. 'It's Poh Sim . . .' As moving a line as I've heard.

The church's silence deepened and held its breath.

Chapter Fifteen

We travelled by boat or coach. The boats, serene and always crowded in that warm summer, nosed down the majestic Rhine at an idle pace which gave us the chance to see the villages and towns, the high perched castles and the immaculate fields. We had been given a cut rate on the boats, yet another example of the Germans' generosity. Everywhere was in such good order. Franz, the coach driver, liked these days. He pushed on ahead of us in his coach with the props and the luggage and had a pleasant chunk of the day to himself, time to find a cafe, time to sink a beer, play dominoes.

The coach was a small mobile suburb. Sometimes we sang, noisily. But we concentrated on the unfolding view of a neat well-heeled Germany, at odds with the bombs and destruction we had seen on news clips, or in the newspapers. I felt a certain bewilderment – that Germany could look so rich – after all that had happened . . . And, probably, there was envy that while in London and other cities we still struggled to clear up the debris and rebuild ports and cities, those we had helped to defeat appeared to be thriving.

We swapped seats a lot. It was the best time to talk to others in the cast. Friendships were begun. There were girls from St Hilda's, always happy to chat; 'Miranda' was as open and innocent as the part she played. One of the girls talked about her dividends which made her seem to be from a foreign country and open to much gentle teasing. The man who played the lead, Prospero, apart from rarely changing his socks, led the chorus of sightseers, notebook in hand, *Diary of a Journey to Germany*. In the rather odd way that seems part of a national character, Ulick and I did not hog each other's company but sought out the empty seat next to one of the rather shy travellers – there was one, Joseph, whom I particularly palled up with.

He came from Manchester and made no attempt to modify his accent. 'I only came here to see Germany,' he said. 'It seemed a cheap way to do it. My dad was in the war. I could never act but they needed somebody to look after the props – I can do that!'

'Would you want to act?'

'Not on your nelly! Same thing night after night? I could read the play twenty times over in that time. No. This is the beginning and end of my theatrical career! It's okay for a short trip. But it's not what you could call serious.'

He had won a major scholarship in mathematics.

He was very proud of Manchester, particularly its orchestra, the Hallé. 'I reckon it's as good as anything you could find in London.'

His family was 'in the clothing trade' and he had doubts about whether to join them or stay on at Oxford and put together a university career.

He was black-haired, vivid in his looks, pecking away at every sight, nodding to himself as if he were drawing up an account.

Did he miss Manchester?

'I do,' he said. 'Some people take a swipe at Manchester but it suits me. You're not supposed to say this, but I think it's got more going for it than Oxford.'
'More what?'
'Life,' he said, and grinned. 'That old thing.'
We were headed for Heidelberg, the crown of German universities.

Usually we stayed overnight en-bloc, in a school or a youth hostel, but at Heidelberg most of us had been consigned to German families. Mine was a professor and his wife, no children, who lived in an impeccable house within easy walking distance of the university. I moved there in the afternoon. From the outset I could see the disappointment in his wife's face. She had been led to believe that a young English gentleman would appear at the door. Instead she opened it to a rumpled, probably rather smelly, long-haired scruff, a peasant.

Her husband was exaggeratedly hospitable. His English was fine, my German non-existent. Embarrassingly, when he showed me some of his precious collection of classics, I attempted to talk in French to make a contribution.

He drove me down to the hall where we were to meet for drinks. I managed to convey that he need not come and fetch me after the event. I could walk back. And, yes, I would very much like to go to his Lutheran church the next morning. And yes, Luther was a great man, a revolutionary man who changed Western civilisation.

It was near the end of the tour and the brakes were slackening. It's fair to say that we had been something of a success and it had rather gone to our heads. The reviews were far too complimentary. In the hall in Heidelberg some

German students had found us. They had brought a glass boot – the size of a riding boot – which they filled and refilled with dark strong beer. It went down a treat. Many toasts were proposed.

'How can you drink that stuff?'

Joseph had asked for a soft drink.

'You should try it.' I heard the slur in my voice but ignored it.

He shook his head. 'You're all turning into caricatures of the Roast Beef John Bull Drunken Englishmen.'

I think I laughed. I was getting brain-soaked on this heavy beer.

Walking back was a touch heroic, I thought, at the time, that is if anything at the time could be described as a thought. But I weaved fairly steadily around the pavements and made the side entrance and shoved in the key I had been loaned. Went upstairs. Must have got into bed. Woke up in the dark being violently, convulsively sick.

It was awful. It was shameful. It was too sudden. I was too enfeebled to make for the lavatory. I put on the light. It was a terrible, horrible, stinking mess.

I tried to clean it up. I tried hard. Used towels, pillow-cases, a bed sheet. Streams of water. Then, back again. Back to bed to dead sleep until the polite knock at the door – time for breakfast.

I have no idea how I negotiated the next stage. Dressing in my spare clothes which scarcely stank. Finding my way to breakfast. Outside I must have seemed reasonably composed if a little pale; inside was an unabatable turbulence threatening another volcanic euption at any moment, as if a broomstick were churning up my guts.

Another World

But the professor got us to the church on time, although I do have a brief but piercing memory of the woman of the house looking at me as if I were something the dog had dragged in. And she had not yet, at that point, seen my room...

My luminous experience of being in a Lutheran chapel listening to the words of the great German Protestant in his own language, a man who changed the Christian world, in a building spare, ascetic, all under control, was memorable. I perspired a lot. The professor was well aware of the dilemma, and smiled, a little nervously, but it was still a smile and it was fixed all the way back in the car.

She was waiting for us. My soiled belongings were tumbling out of a large canvas bag. Thank God I didn't understand German. But there was not the slightest doubt about the subject, the intensity and the disgust of her scorn. And the rage! The rage! The rage! Her husband, as far as I could see, tried his best to offer a defence, an excuse, an olive branch, but this made her even stronger, standing in her door frame, like a Fury. My apologies were sincere, abject, ignored. Who could blame her, I thought, then and since, as that scene flares up in shameful memory, who could blame her? I was rank with indelible remorse and, when I recollect the scene, I still am.

Her husband's suggestion that he drive me back was resisted. But he resisted his wife and we drove back in silence, two sadly apologetic men. We shook hands formally on parting. 'Like gentlemen,' I heard, I swear it. I had let everybody down. I spent the rest of the day sweating and shivering and skulking away from everyone, until the performance.

* * *

On the day we turned back for England, Joseph sought me out. 'Must have been horrible,' he said. He had been a pal.

'It was.'

He paused.

'I'm not coming with the rest of you. It's been a useful way to see Germany. I thought I'd never have the guts to come here . . . but it was helpful being with you all . . .'

'Will you stay here?'

Joseph shook his head.

'I'm moving on to Poland,' he said, 'it has to be done.' His expression was very determined.

I was puzzled. Poland? But I said nothing. Joseph's mood did not lead to further comment. We shook hands.

'There are a lot of Jews in Manchester,' he said and turned away. I saw him brace his shoulders as he walked on. He raised his left arm, still with his back to me. His wave was gentle.

Then the penny dropped.

Chapter Sixteen

Sarah had made a new life. On the first weekends, as she confessed in her letters, she had been 'a bit lost'. 'Impossible,' she wrote, 'to go to a dance on my own, so then what?' She could go to the pictures, she wrote, but most girls she knew were paired up at weekends and her solitary visits to the Palace Cinema in Wigton were not a success. Her father, impressed by her determination to leave school and get a safe job in the bank, let her use his car to practise for her driving test, which she passed first time. She paid for her own lessons and the petrol. Even more generously, when he didn't need the car at weekends, her father was easy about letting her use it. 'I really like driving,' she wrote, 'just driving about from Wigton to Oulton will do. As long as I do no damage he'll let me use it, he says. It's the best present I've ever had.'

It was in the Easter break that the car came into its own. William had passed his test, under conditions from his father similar to those imposed for Sarah. We sought out country pubs some distance from Wigton. David Bland, son of a gentleman farmer whose property was in a neighbouring village to Oulton, had gone to Oxford two years before me – propelled and prepared by Mr James – to read history at Queen's College. He was in his last year. We had seen something of each other at the university, but stronger links came in the vacation, facilitated by the car network. The Kemp brothers, well-off Quakers who lived in a grand house on Station Hill, were also in the car class. David Kemp was an officer in the Royal Navy; and then there was Tom Twentyman, one of four brothers from a farm just outside Wigton. Tom left school at sixteen, joined the police, regretted his choice, came back to school, became a fierce Marxist among all the Cumbrian country farmers and grew a beard. Later he learned Russian, went there and came back even more doubledyed. He was the flint that supplied the spark in any political discussion. Finally there was Alan Powell who had won a scholarship to St Martin's School of Art in London where he thrived. His pencil portraits of the gang of us were the star turn.

David's two sisters would often join us. We usually met at David's house – a fine eighteenth-century farmhouse, whose most attractive characteristic for us was an ample billiard room, and David's sisters who, with Sarah, brought in sandwiches and tea at about nine o'clock on a Saturday night. It was a long way from the Black-a-Moor and I felt that I was playing truant from the pub but Dad said he always had enough staff on a Saturday. I would help out through the week and, most usefully, in the mornings with cellar work before opening time.

The car ensemble was one marker of a new turn in my Wigton's landscape. It was changing. First some of the shopkeepers left their flats above the shops in the middle of the town and built new houses on the fringe of the town. Council houses followed, built on the empty acres which rimmed the old town, a second circle of removal. The old

Another World

town was slowly being hollowed out. Then the better-educated began to desert the town's pubs.

Sour Nook was our out-of-town Saturday drinking spot. An old Victorian pub near Sebergham on a back road into the fells. We had slotted into it very happily. It was a particularly comfortable retreat for me. I was never at ease drinking in Wigton pubs, especially on what could be fractious Saturday nights. Just as Oxford had been a shift away from the town, so Sour Nook. It had a good coal fire; it was never overcrowded. It became a Destination. No singing, no piped music.

Sarah drove me and a couple of others. She blossomed. There was enough farming talk from David and Tom, and plenty of common school references. Sour Nook was a satellite of Wigton, like Oxford.

What we mostly did was argue. With Tom in the company to the Left and the equally combative figure of Alan to the Right, it took very little for gossip to develop into disagreement, to move into head-on argument and to end in 'We'd better drop this before we fall out'.

The question of the atomic bomb and nuclear power on the west coast of Cumbria featured in most general conversations. Did the possession of the atom bomb strengthen or weaken our position in the world? Was the nuclear reactor a few miles away on the west coast more of a menace than a blessing? Talk of the end of the world and poisoning by leakage. I thought the bomb and the peaceful uses of atomic energy were being muddled up. The Aldermaston March protesting against the existence of the bomb was on newsreels and in all the newspapers; famous marchers and a jazz band led the long trail of swelling numbers who made for

Trafalgar Square. The thrill of a popular movement seeking to control the government. 'You will send a British Foreign Secretary naked into the conference chamber,' said Nye Bevan, and would this not give Russia an open goal? I was all for banning the bomb. Sarah was by no means as convinced. Evidence was put on the table from Japan. The fear factor was fanned in that safe country pub. 'It's better than Oxford,' Sarah said, as we drove back. Her tone was approving. Cumberland could beat Oxford at its own game!

As well as working for my father, I helped out on Sarah's farm when need be. This softened her father and mother's view of me although it was still rigid in its essentials. He must have known about the barn, but he never commented. He liked to tease me about Oxford – rather impressed despite the lack of evidence of real work. Sarah went so far as to say that he quite approved of me.

We kept our engagement secret. We bought the ring in Carlisle covered market. I proposed on the bridge over Bassenthwaite Lake next to the Pheasant. Sarah kept it in her purse.

Chapter Seventeen

In Oxford you were largely left to your own devices – to the strength of your character – when it came to study. This, it seemed, was one of the points of the university. After the Prelims, you were unmolested by examinations for two and a half years. Then came Finals. For those two and a half years you could drive or drift as you pleased. It was a time for joining clubs; it was a time for messing about; it was a time to turn whims into habits. It was a time to take a reading on the path you would follow. It was a time to slack.

In those first two terms most of us hurried off to lectures in the morning, to the big halls to listen to distant dons for an hour. Getting there, making notes, getting back could take an hour and a half at least.

For what? We were encouraged by our tutors to be extremely selective. Most of the lecturers delivered information already available in one of their books. So what was the point? One book could cover a dozen lectures. The dons we met were quite prepared to tell you, even encourage you, to avoid this or that lecture; as time went on it seemed increasingly obvious that a book was more useful and relevant.

Like others, I dropped out of many of these public lectures. At first a no-show at lectures felt like truanting. Then, not discouraged by the dons and accepted by many of us, it became a valued shortcut and one in the eye for a mediaeval tradition that had largely outlived its usefulness.

I suspect that the core group of those who turned up to the lectures were themselves preparing for lecturing in their professional future and saw this as an opportunity to pick up tips, as much to copy a style as to receive information.

I thought that those already had their futures sorted out. As had others. Medics would become doctors; lawyers, lawyers; many of the others, teachers or civil servants. The much smaller force of 'don't knows' and even smaller 'don't cares' used it as a holiday, a chance to bask in the sun without getting burnt. There were hard workers, like Robert in his laboratory – the scientists had the strictest routine – and there were the determinedly idle, like Alan. The rest of us got through at our own pace.

It did not do to be too clever, or rather, to seem too clever. Donald Trelford, later editor of the *Observer*, was fond of repeating what he had overheard in the bar of the Randolph Hotel. Referring to Donald, one entitled county person had said, 'He's only here because he's clever.' Some were formidably clever. At that time First Class degrees were few, awarded almost grudgingly. In the history faculty, for instance, there were well over three hundred undergraduates and usually about ten Firsts. A First became the 22-carat mark of intelligence and capability. It was an uncertain measure. Outside the academic arena, Firsts were by no means natural organisers or managers or innovators or leaders. Their remarkable aptitude for memorising relevant clusters of information and passing exams did not automatically transfer into the world of hard knocks. You could even argue that a cloistered three years of swotting was a poor way to prepare for Life. For most non-Firsts that was a plausible comfort.

The rather frantic pace of our early weeks slowed down and the pace of the final weeks was way in the future, beyond our horizon. We were left with the business of getting on with it, for more than two years, of drifting at our own pace. A saunter. A licensed gap, settled in now, firmly established, the second-year cliques in place, pubs sorted out, teams chosen, clubs picked, the comfortable realisation for many that this was It. This meandering, undemanding, cultivated, 'cut above' experience was the Oxford deal. Many thought that swanning around was the best way to spend time, dipping in and out of the many possibilities. Clubs were more pressing than lectures. Solitary work was a pleasant way 'pour passer le temps'.

Save for the exhilarating term spent with the Celtic monks and the impact of early Christianity on the country and its divisions into several independent states at war or threatened by invasion, much of the history I had read at Oxford had already been well served by Mr James back at school.

Here we had a choice of 'special subjects'. In wanting to do the juvenile thing, 'something different', I hovered over the American War of Independence, but finally decided to study the Italian Renaissance. The set books were in Renaissance Italian, the commentaries largely in contemporary Italian. I had not bargained for that. I knew not a word of the language. But the idea of going to Florence, seeing that city of timeless artists, of being in touch with Catholic wars and papal politics, the complex, corrupt and risqué history of the Renaissance all alongside the eye-blinding genius of it all gripped my imagination and, despite warnings from the tutors, I went for it. In the first few weeks I thought my mind was going to split open. Far from taking me to the subject, the new languages – mediaeval and modern Italian – began to paralyse whatever brain survived.

The only advantage I possessed was that I was used to being on my own and concentrating hard.

The first difficulty was to get hold of the book by Guicciardini. The other books on the course – principally Machiavelli's *The Prince* – had bred translations over many years. Guicciardini, the statesman of Florence, the man of civic talents who turned to writing history towards the end of his life, had few translations and of these none were available even in the Oxford libraries by the time I got to them. Such as there had been were out or borrowed. John Hale, a brilliant Renaissance scholar, was my tutor for this subject, which, unfortunately, had become more popular and the end result was that the only way I could get to the books I needed for the time I needed was to go to Senate House, part of the University of London, where not only was Guicciardini's work available but there were books about his book.

I went to London, armed with a note from Professor Hale, and got the books I wanted which had to be returned to the shelves the day after use. I worked there every day for two and a half weeks. The book was essential for basic information for essays about the Renaissance in the 1490s and the early fifteenth century. There would also be gobbets, that is, short extracts of lines which had to be translated into English. It was not a walkover. On some days I was dizzy with it, but there was something approaching excitement. It was new!

Another World

Sarah was in Cumberland. London was a foreign land. I was not flush. The cheapest room for bed and breakfast I could find was in a street uphill behind Victoria Station. The receptionist at Senate House advised me to try that area. The advertisement in the window was irresistibly cheap. The slim dark-haired landlady from Cork, very strict, showed me the room. It was big, on the first floor, two rooms knocked into one. There were three mattresses on the floor with a neat heap of sheets, pillows and blankets on top of them. As the eighteen days grew, so did the number of mattresses. By the time I left there were nine of us. I was the only man not working on a site.

They were Irish, like the landlady and, like her, they were calm and polite. They were just like the lads who came to Wigton to build the Secondary Modern school, returning politeness for politeness, private quiet jokes, sending money back home. On some nights I went out drinking with one or two of them, but I couldn't keep up and I would sidle away after I'd stood my round. Then I walked where my feet took me for the next hour or two. I missed Sarah terribly and phoned her too often for her father and mother's liking. Sarah was interested in what I was doing. Her seriousness on the matter gave me a sense that I was on a mission.

The contrast between the grind of Senate House, the head-spinning recourse to the dictionary and my own stabs at translation, which I always felt were jumping off a cliff into the dark, were somehow balanced by the mattress culture in Victoria, ordinary working life. On my last night half a dozen of us went down to the local pub and drank Guinness which was good and played darts and came back up the street singing together, but not too loudly.

Chapter Eighteen

Waiting for him, I was making a bad shot at being inconspicuous. I walked up and down in front of the College. He had come to Reading with the Cumbrian bowling team which gave us this chance. But for a lack of a military uniform, I could have been guarding the place. I was smoking Disque Bleu, the French cigarettes I had adopted when I worked there for a few weeks before Oxford. They had been cheap, exotic, gave a kick and soon became a habit – *and* available in Oxford. Smoking was more than a mannerism; it helped define a character. I liked offering cigarettes and being offered a cigarette, tasting different brands and picking them out in tobacconists, the shelves as crowded with fags as a sweet shop with sweets. There was a certain social security – you were never alone with a cigarette and the faint pressure of the soft packet of Disque Bleu in the pocket promised instant content and evidence of a generous nature. Films were populated with stars who pulled out a cigarette at crucial moments.

Finally my father came around the corner from Broad Street, a cigarette in his left hand as usual, Capstan Full Strength as always, ambling. He looked around calmly, a wave with his free hand when he saw me waiting for him. His manner, which had been cautious and rather shy, perked up. Again he waved his cigarette hand in my direction and came across to the entrance to the College.

The shyness I had picked up from his manner when I first saw him across the road was more intense when we met.

'So you got the letter,' he said.

'There wasn't time to reply.'

'I knew you'd be here.'

His eyes wandered across the front of the College.

'And this is it.'

'It is.' I laughed. 'The barracks.'

Dad lowered his voice.

'I had a walk through the town . . .' He nodded. 'It makes you think.'

'That's what we're here for.'

We smiled at each other and for a few moments I felt we were stuck there, stuck on the pavement, neither of us knowing what to do, quite content.

'I was at Reading for the bowls,' he said, almost apologetically.

'How did you get on?'

'We got to the quarter-finals. But then there's some good bowlers around. And I thought . . .'

'That you'd come here and say hello. I'm glad you did!'

He nodded, somehow embarrassed.

'We could look around the College,' I said.

He nodded again. 'I'd like that.'

It was early autumn, the beginning of my second year. I'd been allocated a room of my own at the top of Staircase One. Small, an attic, a bit of a hutch but snug. Far easier for work. I thought we might brave that later on but first of all we made a tour. The Chapel where the choir, luckily, was taking its afternoon practice. We stood at the back and listened. I think that the place itself was already working on my father and his intensity of enjoyment matched the choir's rehearsal. The dining hall was being laid for dinner, the long oak tables, the rapid organisation of crockery and cutlery, the gleam from the high polish which caught the rays of the early evening sun, the high rafters. My father was very quiet.

He smiled at the neatness of the lawns; 'your grandfather would have appreciated that'. Dad responded to the two or three nods which came our way from a thin traffic of undergraduates who spotted that this was father and son. Their manners were a silent welcome. The Common Room was too crowded and too complicated to enter. We turned back towards the main quad.

On the way we passed alongside the biggest garden, distinguished by a magnificent copper beech tree. Beyond it was the Fellows' Garden, exclusive to the dons and their guests, and finally, the smallest of all, the Warden's Garden. I described each one on our tour and my father's appreciation broadened. 'You treat yourselves well,' he said. 'It reminds me of a house I once worked in, it was alongside Ullswater, a beautiful place, very grand. Your Aunty Mary and Aunty Elsie worked there and got me a start as a boots boy. The two places here have a similar feel to them.'

Mr Stone came out of the Senior Common Room as we made for the gate. He stopped as soon as he saw us. 'This is my father,' I said. 'And this is Mr Stone, one of the tutors. He does history.'

Lawrence held out his hand. He was taller than my father.

'I've heard something about you,' my father said. 'He' – he nodded at me – 'has a very high opinion of you. He says you're hard to please.'

Mr Stone laughed. 'I'm on the way for a cup of tea in my rooms. Would you like to join me?'

Dad gave me a quick glance – for permission, I guess. I nodded. Dad said, 'I'd like that.'

Lawrence Stone's room was smack above the entrance porch, accessed by a narrow spiral of stone steps which led to a wonderful octagonal-shaped room in which we received our teaching. Mr Stone did his research and writing here. It was a unique room with a double aspect. One set of tall windows looked out into the front quad and the other out into a street which led down to Wren's Sheldonian. The founders of the Royal Society in 1660 had assembled there in what was then Christopher Wren's room. He had designed the magnificent Sheldonian Theatre in Oxford, as well as St Paul's Cathedral in London. When I had first walked into that room, small as it was, I had felt much the same as when I walked into a cathedral or a country church. The same hush with all the layers of worship. Now, with my father, I felt doubly moved.

I realised then, and if not then soon afterwards, that there had been a change in how my father and I saw each other.

Until then, I had been protected by him and looked up to him. He led. That day it was his nervousness that cued me. My father, with a glance, a gesture, a tone in his voice, now relied on me to get through this; at first. He soon relaxed. I felt it then as I feel it now, a pride in him and a sadness.

I saw his scan of the bookshelves in the historic and lovely room. I thought I could hear him think. Later he said to me, 'I would just like to have sat down and been able to read anything I wanted, just to be in a place like that and read those books.' I saw that gaze, not of envy, but wonder that there were lives that could be lived like this and his son was part of it. Mr Stone's unaffected kindness and the resonance of the room on which Mr Stone had delivered a brief history had transported my father into a different world. He would never forget that visit. This was, for him, a perfect place partly because it was for me but also because he knew, in a way he had not known before, that this place, the books, the scholarly attention of Mr Stone represented a world he had never even dreamt of and would never encounter again. And I was living it.

Dad soon pulled himself together and relaxed. I can still 'see' that but I can also 'see' the look he gave me. A modest smile of such pride and happiness for me. It was fleeting but unforgettable. Soon he picked up the poise and openness which made him such a well-loved man. But a change had been made between us.

* * *

Mr Stone poured the cups of tea and brought them over to the small table beside the sofa where my father and I were rather uncomfortably poised.

Mr Stone had alluded to his time in a submarine in World War II. 'It was thought to be out of reach of the Germans,' he said.

'I worked at a place called Kirkbride before the war started,' my father said, bucked up by the reference Mr

Stone had made to the war. 'That was considered way off the beaten path and damaged planes would hedge-hop to there often from Kent. We fettled them up to make them serviceable for re-entry into action. It was an aeroplane hospital. It was a reserved occupation but I signed up after a few months.'

'There's no doubt that in those early years it was the Air Force that held the line,' Mr Stone said. 'I'm not terribly fond of all Churchill's tub-thumping, but when he said "never have so many owed so much to so few", he had a point. A friend of mine is writing about the Polish pilots who became part of the RAF. As always, a mixture of high adventure, heroics and bungling. Did your son give you some idea of this place?'

'He did. Except what goes on is what goes on in their heads really, isn't that all that matters?'

'I'll suggest to the Warden that he hires you!' Mr Stone smiled.

'But I wonder' – Dad was settled in – 'what relevance does most of what they learn here have on what they do afterwards.'

Mr Stone smiled; he had a sweet smile tinged with a twinkle of mischief.

'We can't really solve that one,' he said. 'We teach teachers to teach as we were taught. And doctors. Scientists go on to bring health to the world – and historians . . .' He looked at me and laughed. 'In some cases the best we can hope for is that we have lined their minds.'

'Do you really believe that, Mr Stone?'

'I do. I believe that any serious discipline properly pursued will train and organise the mind and could improve a life.'

'How do you know when you've done that?'

I was a little uneasy at Dad's persistence. Mr Stone was completely unfazed.

'I don't think we can, definitively. They get better at exams. Is that very important?' He paused. 'We don't know. They store more knowledge, but even then what great advantage is there of turning the brain into a library? Why not just reach out for a book, and find the necessary text? Why not leave the mind alone to play its own games as it does with the great poets and musicians and philosophers? There's no answer.'

Both my father and myself were struck by and to some extent struck dumb by Mr Stone's amiable line of persuasive argument.

'What's learning for then?' my father asked.

The tutor laughed.

'If I knew that, I'd be a rare bird. Obvious learning is in knowing where countries are, what languages people speak, how to build a house, how to plough a field, on and on we could go about what we learn. And need to learn. And want to learn. Perhaps we are the learning species. Perhaps that's the key to all we are. But it's what you do with this learning that matters. A little learning can be dangerous, they say, but a little learning can also breed a new encyclopaedia of knowledge. And knowledge can come and indeed has come from here, there and everywhere. We are just some of the temporary custodians.'

***

'Does he talk like that all the time?' my father asked, as we walked along to the pub.

'A bit. But not quite like that. I think he was just enjoying himself and hoped that you were.'

'I certainly was. Wonderful being able to listen to a man like that every day.'

My father was silent for a few moments. I responded for him.

'He wants, I don't know how to say it, to open things up, to make us think harder or in a different way, and even play games just to show what's possible.'

'Well, I'll never forget it,' said my father. 'I'll make sure never to forget it. He made me see what it's all about, that's for certain . . . for certain. What a good man!'

We went into the pub next door. I had hoped that Ulick, Robert or Alan might be there but no luck. Still, even at this early hour it was almost full.

'It runs itself, a place like this,' my father said, looking around. 'I bet these lads come in most nights. No trouble. Steady trade. Pleasant talk. A pub in Oxford would be a walkover.'

We went down Broad Street, past Trinity College and Balliol, crossing the road at the Martyr's Memorial to go by the Randolph towards Worcester College and then on to the railway station, Dad looking around constantly and always with an expression of pleasure as if it said, 'This is the place and what a place this is.'

He would take the train to Reading Station where the coach was detailed to pick up the Cumbrian bowlers at 9 p.m. and travel back north.

I did not intend to, but at the last minute I got on the train with him. When we reached Reading we went over to the waiting coach.

A warm night. The right end to the day. Dad reached out to shake my hand.

'Who'd have thought it?' he said, and repeated, 'who'd have thought it?' There was that moment of pause – how should we part? There was the slightest tremor in his voice – which I caught.

My father pulled out his packet of Capstan. 'Have one of mine for a change,' he said. 'It'll do you good.'

Chapter Nineteen

The Joint Action Committee Against Racial Intolerance (JACARI) was established in my time at the university. It was an immediate success. Within a couple of years it became the biggest club in the university, a bigger membership than the Union. There was a commitment about it which gave it clout. It was not just another Oxford club; it was an international crusade. The anti-apartheid movement took a grip on this country. South Africa, for those who regarded the Empire as sacred and still thought of it as part of the United Kingdom's reach on the world's map, was in some moral way seen as a responsibility.

It is increasingly difficult to credit that this small offshore island of Europe still claimed sovereignty over such a mighty land mass. I had a pencil sharpener in the shape of a globe with the functional end in the Antarctic. If you spun it fast enough you could see a continuous governing blur of pink – Britain, the Empire. On which the sun never set. It was heady stuff. And this was after the 'loss' of North America. We were still, in the forties and fifties, expected to be proud of the Empire, to police it, to Anglicise its laws, to reorganise its civil services and communication systems – especially the railways – and to plant English and the King James Bible as the key language of administration and faith.

It was an extraordinary, bold, an outrageous, even dangerous, enterprise dependent on the army and navy of a small nation and the driving force of the Industrial Revolution. Looking back it was bewildering and yet, for some decades, successful in its appropriations. The Empire was now beginning to creak and threaten to break up. Yet it still reserved the right to govern, or at least to influence, vast parts of the world it had seized. Its insistence on supporting a brutal Black and white divided South Africa was seen by many British people as an affront to the ideals of the Empire. To be challenged. To be rubbed out if not by arms then by arguments, demonstrations and international obloquy.

There was a general committee for JACARI to which I belonged. One of its sub-sections was a group determined to show solidarity with the Black South Africans by setting up a scholarship for a student to come to Oxford. The money was raised, permission was given by the College authorities, we persuaded Wadham College to house the newcomer, and Jeppe May arrived on a two-year scholarship.

Jeppe was amiability itself. We learned that he was married, with two children. He was to read history. The scholarship was not extravagant, not even particularly generous, as I remember, but thought to be sufficient and the glass was always half full for Jeppe. He had rooms of his own in the new quad. I can remember no incident nor any reported incident of prejudiced behaviour. Of course it could have been masked.

Oxford at the time would not have been without prejudice. Like every British town and city there was resentment of Black immigrants, which could lead to any number of snubs, derogatory remarks, fights, attacks. There was, among some, a still indelible belief in the white man's God-given superiority. God was 'portrayed' as white, the devil as black. Geography was not brought into the equation. Nor was climate. Nor was common sense.

It was clear that despite his fortitude Jeppe did not find it easy. The few other people of colour in the Oxford mix were rich and set on a track to becoming successful back in their home country after the Oxford Experience. Jeppe had struggled from a modest background and now found himself apparently crowned with this scholarship but cut off from his roots, his family and his breathing space. Moreover the way in which history was taught at this English university, both the content and the method, were alien to him. Studying the Wars of the Roses or the Civil War, the Reform Act or the Chartist movement was like chasing shadows. Nor was he accustomed to the layering required in the essays. Mr Stone found a way to deal with this and he drew up a plausible alternative work-table which would help Jeppe get a degree, discount any humiliation and give the man a chance in this foreign world.

Jeppe knew all that. We knew he knew it. What did help was contact with a lot of people – by the end of his first year his beaten-down air had dissolved.

* * *

About this time my parents decided to leave Wigton and move south, to a pub in Reading, the Plasterers Arms, in Newtown, just short of where the Kennet Canal flowed into the Thames. Huntley & Palmers' biscuit factory was on one side and a mighty gasworks dominated the other.

It was my father's impulsive move, momentous for my mother, but after their failure (rather, her failure) to move to Workington, where he had been offered a much better pub, she had said she would not stand in the way of any next move and she kept her word. Dad had come across the pub in the few days he had spent in the bowling tournament in Reading at the Island Club. The place had caught his fancy. He had never been adhesively sealed into Wigton. He had arrived there in his late teens from West Cumbria, the mining strip which went under the sea. His own father had worked there.

One of Reading's attractions for him was this bowling green. And Reading itself was fresh.

Bowls was now my father's sport. Horses were for his gambling days. Hound trails, central to the existence of his pub in Wigton, were confined to the north. Bowls took up his interest.

He was good. He had played for Cumberland a couple of times and, a year or so after he arrived in Reading, he played for Berkshire. The Island Club had an exclusivity and a quaintness which appealed to him. And being rowed across a stretch of the Thames to get to the green never ceased to please him. He took me a few times and it was as if he were the boy being thrilled and I the only mildly impressed adult. It had a singular character that made him feel special.

I had bought him a set of bowls for a birthday, the first decent present I'd bought him. They had his initials inscribed on both sides of the gleaming black carefully weighted woods, much the same as Drake had used when the Spanish Armada was in the English Channel threatening to wipe out Elizabeth I once and for all. Though informed that the Spanish galleons were approaching in force, Drake reportedly said, 'We have time to finish our game and go on and defeat the Spanish fleet.'

My grandfather, after a bad pit accident, had totally changed tack and was Wigton's Park Keeper for the latter span of his life. The Wigton Bowling Green was his pride. I was allowed to use the light roller from time to time and I was also allowed to trim the edges of the Green. The Park Green was twice selected for county games. The grass looked and felt like velvet. The rinks were pre-measured to the inch with pegs and string before the final, concentrated light mowing.

The graceful, shallow curve as the bowl swung out and then in again seeking the jack. Then the click of the bowls as one dislodged the opponent's bowl but stopped right up against an unmoved white jack. The nuances, the time to destroy, the bending of the knee to deliver the bowl – did that have a historical precedent too? The apparent ease meeting the greatest difficulty in placing the swerving bowl so accurately that it could gain a point and upset the opponent's game. A quiet solitary skill. All over the land. My father loved the game. I was never much good at it.

So the move south clicked for him. Charlie Allardyce, a friend of Dad's, drove them down to look at the pub – which was advertised for re-tenanting – and he, too, expressed his admiration. It sat big among the rows of small terraced housing of Newtown, on the edge of Reading, a mile or so's walk, or a bus ride, to the centre. My mother thought it was old-fashioned – surprised that the south should not be ahead of the north. The pub had a capacious bar, and an even bigger saloon bar which sported a darts board. There was no singing room. The kitchen was part of a flat upstairs. There was a snug.

The snug was small, two benches against opposing walls, a door that led out to the passage which served as a short-cut from our street to the next. The fourth side was the bar.

The snug's regular inhabitants were local women, elderly, friends it seemed from schooldays, who had adopted it as their club. Some of them brought mugs and flagons. The flagons were filled with mild ale by my father, who gave them a generous pint measure which they fed into their mugs carefully as the evening went on. After an hour or so they would get their flagons refilled and set off back to their nearby houses for a comfortable evening in front of the television. Something about their clannish character engaged my father and they took to him and teased him. The snug was prone to sudden loud outbursts of laughter.

Although there were snugs in one or two Wigton pubs, Dad thought that there was something attractively antiquated about this particular setup. Probably it was the flagons that did it. Planted on the bar to be filled up. Tucked under the bench to be reached for when the mug ran dry – and there were those who came into the snug with their flagon but 'couldn't stay', 'had to get back', and once again the flagon-filling routine was called into action. Mild beer was cheaper than bottled and, Dad said, 'They know they'll get more for their money in one of those big jugs of theirs.' He enjoyed being slightly conned by the manoeuvre but most of all he enjoyed the talkative elderly ladies, their appropriation of the snug as their private lair, and the jar or flagon which, he said, 'took him back to the old pubs when his father would go out after work of an evening with a sixpence and bring back a jar.'

I spent only short bursts at the Plasterers Arms. I was proud of how my mother buckled down. Wigton had been her cradle, her school and in its way her passion. All left behind. The intense companionships, the meetings in the streets, the shops, the dances, the outings, the layers of memory. In Wigton she could not take a step without meeting her former self. Now she had been uprooted, and ripped from memories that had fed her conversation and nourished her history. But Reading Newtown?

Where were the familiar faces in the streets? Where the nudges from the past, the weaving of the past with the present? All gone. She must have missed it; she referred to it now and then but she did not mourn. The pub became the motor, its people her people, and small connections grew. She had given my father her word and she kept it. No apparent regrets, no sulking, an appreciation of the new way of life she had been landed with and that, as far as I could tell, was the sum of it.

My father had moved around all his life. From school to a farm as a boy labourer, to a Big House as a boots boy, to a brief time in the mines, to a factory in Wigton, a time in the steel works at Scunthorpe, then to Kirkbride aerodrome in a reserved occupation, from there into the forces and post-war back to the factory; he moved from one to the other, also taking up part-time jobs – collecting insurance, working as a bookie – alongside the full-time occupation. He made friends easily, remembered names, happily did favours, was always and remained popular in a way that even as a teenager I envied. He was good at making brief but convincing speeches when the occasion called for them. And, even more than my mother, he enjoyed company. I suppose that coming from a family of nine, it was part of his make-up. The Island Bowling Club gave him constant pleasure.

There was also a sense, which he hinted at, that whereas the Black-a-Moor was Ethel's Wigton domain, he had at least an equal stake in Reading.

When I asked why they had made such a dramatic move south, there was a certain embarrassment from my father and no useful information from my mother.

I guessed that he had been hankering after change for some years and the Island Bowling Club was the key to opening the door. Was that enough to move more than two hundred miles south to a place neither of them knew and had never visited? A sudden impulse? A dash for freedom from his wife's (and his son's) Wigton grip? More income? I never asked him that. It remains an odd move. Perhaps the answer was simple and would have been given had I asked. Just another of the several questions I regret I didn't ask my parents about their lives. My room was at the top of the pub flat, self-contained, with a sink, a coal fire and a view across the rooftops to the biscuit factory of Huntley & Palmers on one side and that sweep of the River Thames flanked by the two gasometers on the other.

My father took to it. The customers were local, working and artisan class, keen on dominoes and darts when a space could be cleared in the saloon bar. This proved to be a lifeline for my mother. In Wigton, with very rare exceptions, women did not play darts. In Reading, they did. The pub's landlady was expected to captain the women's darts team. There were well-organised leagues.

Another World

My mother, who had scarcely pitched a dart in the Black-a-Moor in Wigton, took on the responsibility and – fairy tale! – proved to have a flair for it. She was Landlady of the Year twice on the trot. The final was in a ballroom with a band and an M.C. I was very proud of her. She refused to enter after that. But her prowess settled her and gave her a link with the customers. Dad's improvement of the quality of the draught beer which benefited from his rigorous daily cleaning of the pumps and his general tidiness got him good marks. He was soon at home.

Just as in the north, it was a time when pubs were social centres. I helped behind the bar at the Plasterers when I was at our new home. That soon broke you in to the community but I have only the merest memories of the customers. Even today, aged 86, I can go through the bar of the Black-a-Moor society more than seventy years ago. The Plasterers has left no such indelible memories.

The best of Reading for me was walking along the towpath, by the Thames, to Sonning. It had been nominated for the loveliest village in England, glamorous houses nesting up an easy slope, the lock with the expensive good-looking private boats moored nearby and the spice of living celebrities – even film stars – who had bought houses there. For my mother, the traipse along the often muddy towpath was worth every step. She would then wander around this village paradise.

* * *

I never witnessed a fight in the pub in Reading, but my father said there had been 'trouble' once or twice. He liked the customers and there was more money than in the north.

He bought my mother an expensive jacket on which she clipped the brooches he also bought along the way. It was a bit showy, she thought, but she would sometimes wear it on Saturday evenings. One Saturday in autumn, somebody got through the house door, raided the upstairs and went off with it. 'That's the end for me of jewellery,' she said.

I sought out Reading Gaol and just stared at it. How could Oscar Wilde willingly condemn himself to be imprisoned there? He is praised by many people for his heroic decision to face up to the charge of homosexuality which in his day was criminal, feared and practised quite freely at Oxford then as now. In a poem he wrote about 'the love that dare not speak its name'. But looking at the place – why did he not take the opportunity he was given to flit to Paris? There must have been an overweening heroic streak in him or the obstinate determination not to be bullied or perhaps in some self-tormented way he thought he deserved punishment for what he had done? Whatever it was, I went to stare at the prison to try to imagine that gilded bird in that cruel cage. That it had actually happened *there*.

Or was he simply unaware of the brutal conditions waiting for him?

* * *

I invited Jeppe to come and stay in Reading for a few days, beginning the day after New Year. I met him at the station and we walked to the pub, alongside the Kennet Canal, unremarked. I knew no one we passed on the street. Nor did he.

My mother had sorted out the spare bedroom, put fresh flowers in a vase beside the bed. An electric kettle with a tin of coffee was next to the wash basin. As soon as he had settled in, Jeppe asked if he could go out for a stroll into the town. He had read about Oscar Wilde and wanted to see the prison. What was clear was that he wanted to be alone, to taste the temperature of the town on his own terms. I sympathised with that and with my mother I stood in the doorway waving him off. It was a very cold day.

It was there that I began to get a measure of the strain he was enduring.

I guess that readers already take it for granted that my parents would like Jeppe. Who, save a bigot, wouldn't? He was shy, charming, good-mannered, thoughtful... He had met some people from Reading at a Revivalist meeting in Oxford, he said, and they had invited him to look them up if ever he came to the town.

It was not a great time for racial harmony in England. The university section of Oxford could be thought an exception. But at that time some of the newspapers were relentless in printing the worst. I fretted about Jeppe on his walk and from my eyrie room kept an eye on the road back from the town. He appeared a couple of hours later, when it was all but dark. I saw him, his stroll, the rolling shoulders, seemingly at ease with the world, in and out of the street lights, distinctive by the warm Wadham College scarf my mother had insisted he wear on the cold day. He was as usual, as in Oxford, ambling, apparently unperturbed by any possible attacks which I feared might be in wait. He came into the pub. I guessed he would go into the bar – it was just past opening time, a few regulars. I went downstairs to be with him.

'You needn't have worried,' he said. I hadn't spoken a word. 'A half of bitter please, Mrs Bragg. And you?'

'The same.'

'And crisps. Salted. Thank you.'

We went into an empty side of the room, near to the fire. He was shivering.

'My friends wanted to show me the prison,' he said.

'Oscar Wilde?'

'Was anybody else ever in it? . . . Cheers. I can see you were worried about me.'

I nodded.

'My friends had some stories . . . they say it's everywhere but Reading seems okay. At the moment. If you know where not to go.'

'Where not to go?'

'Yes. Just keep your eyes open.' He raised his glass. 'Where to go is not so hard. You find out where other Black people go and follow the trail!' He laughed. 'Jungle lore.'

'I suppose all of us do that in one way or another,' I said.

He let it pass.

We went upstairs. Jeppe was still cold despite the fire. He took a bath. I talked with my mother.

'It's such a shame,' she said, 'you couldn't come across a nicer man.' Her tone was sad. 'When will we get over this kind of thing?'

'It's worse in America, so they say, the slavery, even now.'

'That doesn't make it any better here. I suppose it's always been like that.'

'It hasn't.' I dug into the history I was being taught. 'The Romans had a Black Emperor.'

My mother nodded. She was unconvinced, as I myself was.

'We took slaves to America,' she volunteered. 'Didn't we? We were always part of it.'

Her distress was visible. Jeppe's visit had raked up a rarely expressed passage from her history lessons.

'Why do you think it's like that?'

I didn't know.

My mother wanted more. I tried.

'I suppose that whenever one tribe thought they could get advantage of another and take their land or their cattle or their women – they just went ahead and did it,' I said. 'People like us Europeans had an advantage in weapons and found that they were able to wipe out enemies and after that did it again and again, for greed and power. There were slaves in Africa before we went there. And Africans brought their slaves to the European boats on the shoreline standing off ready to make for America in those terrible conditions. But yes, we did it because we could do it and then there was no looking back – and it was White Men Good, Black Men Bad. We thought God was white, so was Jesus Christ.' It was awkward bringing in the words 'Jesus Christ'. Somehow God was easier to put in the sentence.

My mother hesitated. She was used to brief discussions at Labour Party meetings and not afraid of explaining her point of view. But Black–white, with Jeppe upstairs . . . ?

'I read somewhere,' she said extremely carefully, 'that Jesus Christ might have been a Black person.'

'Where was that?'

She shook her head. 'A magazine. It just stuck.' But she would not be deterred. 'It makes some sense if you think of geography.' Then, 'I never liked geography,' she added.

'There was too much of it. And you couldn't say that in Wigton.'

'Do you miss Wigton?'

She hesitated for a truthful moment.

'I'm getting used to it here,' she said. 'They're nice people. And it's a change.'

Her expression did not match the words . . .

After supper, Jeppe and I went into the saloon bar. This was usually my mother's terrain with a waitress serving those who did not want to go up to the bar itself. It had sofas – second-hand but serviceable – a dart board: the calm pitching, a low thud of the arrows, the murmured scores, not unlike a sect about their ritual, ignoring everyone else and ignored by them.

A few minutes after Jeppe and myself went into the saloon bar, my father swapped bars with my mother and came to watch over Jeppe.

What distinguished the saloon bar on Sunday evenings was a quartet of Welsh women who came in – about eight o'clock – for a few drinks together and a sing-song. Mainly hymns. One of them, Gwyneth, had a strong Welsh soprano voice which carried along the other three as if she were driving horses, whipping them on, steering the hymn. Provided it did not go on too long, it was tolerated by most of the customers and actively appreciated by a core of regulars who came for the show as much as the company.

Jeppe was relaxed, smiling behind his glass of bitter, as contented as I'd seen him. Mostly, I think, because of the affectionate attentions of the women who knitted him into their conversation without patronage or prejudice.

'Do you sing much where you come from?'

'A lot,' said Jeppe. 'Sometimes we would all – all the village – sit around a fire at this time of year and watch a pig being roasted and sing our old songs now and then.'

'Would we know your old songs?'

'I don't think so.' He smiled. He had such a natural smile. 'But sometimes we would sing hymns just like you do. Sometimes the same hymns. We learned them at the Mission School and sang them – hymns – like you do, on Sundays.'

'*Our* hymns?'

Jeppe smiled. ' "Bread of Heaven" was our favourite,' he said, and the Welsh women applauded. He never put a foot wrong.

'Our hymns too,' he said, and laughed. 'Everybody's hymns. One God for all of us.'

'He's right! Do they dance as well?' The questioner underlined her point by waving her arms.

'That's it!' he said obligingly.

I had entered the bar with some apprehension. The influx from the West Indies, especially those who had been encouraged to come to Britain to find work, homes and prosperity, had often met with brutal hostility. 'Pinching Our jobs'. 'Taking over Our streets . . .'

Of what happened on the evenings Jeppe spent in the Plasterers Arms, I can testify that nothing inflammatory was heard. There may have been murmurs of 'darkie' or 'them coming over here and taking over . . .' Was there a mood among some which Jeppe sensed and we avoided sensing? If so he glided through it and from his expression and his occasional quiet laughter, seemed to be enjoying it. More as the night wound towards closing time and my father called out: 'Last orders! Last orders ladies and gentlemen please! Time please!'

'We always ended,' said Jeppe, taking the lead for the first time, 'by singing "Abide With Me".'

'We sing that at Wembley. At the Cup Final,' one of the men said. The serendipity of the coincidence appeared to loop everyone together.

'We sing that as well,' said Gwyneth. 'Sometimes in Welsh.' She paused. 'Why don't you start us off, Jeppe?'

For a moment it seemed to me that an unfair weight had been planted on Jeppe's good nature.

He took a deep breath and somehow most of us in the pub knew what was happening. Much of the room quietened down and the darts players pitched even more murmurously.

Abide with me, fast falls the Eventide,
The darkness deepens, Lord with me abide.
When other helpers fail and comforts flee
Help of the helpless, Lord, abide with me . . .

Without a pause, he continued:

'I fear no foe . . .' and took up through the second verse. And then the final one, by which time the room was quiet. 'In life, in death, O Lord, abide with me.'

He was no Paul Robeson, but nor was he shy and those words came so warm and calm into the pub. It was the intensity, the passion that caught us all. He was singing this hymn for his homeland, however English it seemed, for his own past, no matter the difference of those who were his audience now. He meant it. And we understood that. And without extravagance but with open appreciation, he got a round of applause.

Cigarettes were offered. But he didn't smoke. An encore was requested but the blanket of shyness was drawn back over him.

'You have a lovely voice,' said my mother when we had tea in the kitchen afterwards. 'Even in the bar they stopped talking. Most of them.'

* * *

The last time I went to the Plasterers Arms was in September 1961. With Alan and Michael I stayed at the pub for the night. It was handy for the CND march in the morning. Both of them were more than happy to be in such down-to-earth company and there were bedrooms enough to have one each. Michael insisted on walking alongside the Kennet Canal down to the Thames in the flickering, inadequate street lighting. There was a sense in which Michael soaked up darkness and was excited by the prospect of any incident along the way that might turn out to be exceptional.

The morning was an early breakfast and a brisk walk to where the nuclear disarmament army was camped with its hundreds of tents in fields beside the Thames. Students were in the majority. The music had stopped after – we were told – what had been a night of dancing. Now we were ready to join the march which had begun at Aldermaston, site and symbol of the new incarnation of the devil – the atomic bomb. The Campaign for Nuclear Disarmament was at its peak. Reading was Leg Two of the march on London.

Those massed tents beside the river and the early morning listlessness of the thousands of young people gave it the smack of a festival, a mood foreign to the gravity of what was happening. I had been on demonstrations with JACARI after the Sharpeville massacre. Jeppe had joined us on that just before he returned to Africa, where he would eventually become headmaster of a school. We wrote to each other. JACARI was growing steadily and tracking the apartheid issue closely. But this BAN THE BOMB movement had seized the headlines. Perhaps it was the directness of the message and the reasonable possibility that something could be and would be done by these mass marches which could and would save the planet from an inferno.

There was gaiety, a sense of carnival. It was the music of Johnny Dankworth and his Jazz Band (jazz, of course; 'classical' would have been too solemn; 'rock and roll' would have been considered too lightweight in those days; jazz hit the button). And we *had* a bomb. We could *do* something. We were still at the Top Table, hanging on by our fingertips but still a player with the resonance of Churchill as yet unfaded. Yes, we would certainly see the Bomb Banned.

Alan had by then moved well away from Wadham and was not only settled in the BBC but building up a successful song-writing company with his old school friend Ken Howard. He hadn't changed a bit. Not in shape (plump), not in manner (thoughtful), nor dress (rather clerical) nor in his conversation (careful, as if he were forever munching through classical poetry to find new lyrics for the pop songs that had become his agenda).

The band started up with 'When the Saints Go Marching In'. We sang along. We straggled forth. One of the world's great philosophers – Bertrand Russell – was at the front, alongside Michael Foot, the famously forthright Labour MP, and Canon Collins, asserting the Church's place on the march for peace. These and others were to stand on the plinth in Trafalgar Square at the foot of Nelson's Column and urge us on as the thousands of marchers came to a crowded halt in Central London and tried to squeeze into the inadequate space. There were no riots. For an occasion concerned with the End of the World and being prepared for that eventuality by several stellar speakers, it was remarkably uphearted.

Somehow we felt we were at the centre of what mattered. The newspapers splashed on it. The march was on radio and television. To have been on an Aldermaston March was to have earned a stripe. We felt virtuous.

Having squeezed into Trafalgar Square to hear the speeches, we eventually managed to squeeze out again. Alan guided us to a small bar in Soho. 'This was where skiffle started in London,' he said, when we came to the Two Eyes, as if showing us the crown jewels.

'Let's go in.'

It was about half full. The clientele exclusively young, rather dashingly though cheaply dressed, sipping lager, absorbed in the stream of pop music from the jukebox. Live performances would begin later. Alan ordered the by now compulsory half of lager.

We sat down near a loudspeaker. Alan nodded along to the music and launched on one of his sermons.

'This is where the cutting edge of culture is now,' he said. 'Not in Oxford. That's a high-class museum, a quaint reminder of the past. Not in the classical music feed on the Third Programme. Good, even matchless as some of it is, its dynamic is done. Jazz, soul, blues, spirituals and above all rock and roll give us the soundtrack to our time – new sounds, from the masses not from the aristocratic courts. And music *for* the masses. Technology has now given the masses a voice. Music is no longer the province of the aristocrats or those who want to climb on board the great game. This' – he pointed to the loudspeaker, Elvis Presley was singing 'All Shook Up' – 'this is Now, it describes who we are TODAY.' He smiled. 'I've written a piece about it and sent it to *The Times*. I have hopes that they'll print it.'

Alan's father wrote occasional essays for the court page of *The Times*. This was Alan's third attempt to follow in his footsteps. 'But of course like most things now, like the novel in its day, for example, it takes time to be accepted. It begins as a minority underground thing and thankfully, in some ways popular music has stayed there. Disapproved of by the elite. That's what you want. I just hope it never becomes established, which could happen. That is the greatest danger . . .'

He raised his glass. 'Cheers. To everything outside respectability. Painting as well as music, writing of course, everything that moves and makes movement.' More Presley came through the loudspeakers. 'There you have it,' said Alan. 'Presley could have been educated and trained to be a fine opera singer. No opera singer could ever be Presley. Instinct can't be taught and pop music at its best is fed by instinct in the music and in the lyrics and in the performance. Here ends today's lesson!' We raised our glasses in a salute.

Later in his life Alan was to suffer a long illness but that flow never stopped. He wrote a book mainly composed of footnotes and always the mixture of erudition, slight preachiness and raciness, even at times licentiousness. The footnotes were the meat of it. Always delivered in unblemished prose.

We had a second lager and crisps. 'I know a place near here,' said Alan, 'rather better than this. You might like to come along. If you don't like it we can leave. It's very casual.'

'I have a train to catch to Reading,' I said.

Alan nodded and sipped the warm pale ale. It was clear he wanted to be off.

'Okay. We'll go right away.'

I bolted down the beer, took a handful of crisps and we were in the maze of Soho. The narrow slits between cafes, the riddle of tightly pressed buildings were familiar. Wigton was like that. We went down a particularly narrow street, dark, litter-laden, unpleasant, more an alley. Alan led, we went in single file. He spoke into a microphone on the door and we were admitted. 'It's illegal, you know,' said Alan proudly. 'That's the fun of it.'

It was like a stage set. Dark turned to light, dozens of carefully placed coloured bulbs, velveteen sofas, saucy prints on the Sherwood green walls, a small dancing area, a disco discreetly operated by an intense youth with a heap of blond hair. There was a bar, two young men serving behind it. Alan smiled encouragingly as we went towards the bar. The singer was repeating 'Honey, honey, honey, I want your honey'. Alan stopped, rather dramatically, turned face on to me and pronounced, 'Honey, in this context, always means sex. Like sugar.' The last word came out emphatically. 'It's only marginally more acceptable than "baby". They should say sex. Sex is perfect . . .' He ordered two glasses of lager – twice as expensive as those we had consumed before. We found a deep dark green sofa and plumped down.

'Cheers!' said Alan, and raised his glass.

My echo was rather weak. There was a lot to take in.

'Experience,' Alan said abruptly. 'All pleasurable experience is valuable. It shores up the spirits and feeds the mind.'

He sipped the lager. So did I. Then I grimaced.

Alan enjoyed that.

'They put a sort of flavouring in it,' he said. 'I thought you'd like it.'

I looked at the glass as if it had been sent to drug me. A young man came across and held out both arms.

I looked at Alan.

'I think he's asking if you'd like a dance,' Alan said, as colourlessly as he could.

A bomb went off in some hitherto unignited area of my brain.

The young man said, 'You're university students, aren't you? I can always tell.'

And again the arms went out inviting a warm embrace. 'I'm Julian,' he said.

My throat was so dry I could have struck a match in it.

'I have a train to catch to Reading,' I said.

The young man hesitated and then laughed.

'Well,' he said, 'I thought I'd heard them all . . . Maybe later, then, when the ice cap has melted.' And off he waltzed.

'You handled that very well,' said Alan. 'He can be a bit of a nuisance.' Later, on the train, I thought – but women dance with women, don't they? 'Would you like another . . . before . . .' Alan's good manners made him stumble.

'Before I go to Paddington? Yes, I would. But no perfume.'

Alan almost concealed his smile as he levered himself out of the sofa and joined the crowd at the bar . . .

Paddington Station was suffocatingly full of the debris from the March. Abandoned 'Ban the Bomb' placards occupied the ground, making a mess of the place. By careful manoeuvring I managed to get on to the correct platform. Guards were at the train doors, police strategically placed. There were police dogs. The tannoy announced the train's departure and those of us next to the first-class carriages were ready to give up. We were not first class. But a heave of bodies pushed the guards to one side and about half a dozen of us managed to tumble into the train. We were next to the lavatory. I went in and locked it and ignored the knocking on the door until the train was under way. Now and then I pulled the chain for a sound effect. After a few minutes I opened the door, as if I were giving myself up. An elderly man pushed past me. He was in a dark three-piece rustic suit enlivened by a flowing silk pocket handkerchief. He repeated rapidly, 'Thank God! Oh dear! Oh dear! Thank God! Thank God!' I mixed in with the other dodgers and made it to Reading sardined but without incident.

I had picked up an *Evening Standard*. The morning march from Aldermaston saturated the coverage. The photos showed a crowd en fête – Nelson's Column stood like a statue to peace rather than a memorial of war. I walked back through Reading feeling that a job had been well done.

Of course the world could be saved.

We were on our way!

Chapter Twenty

'You mean I have to drive across *that*?'

'It's the only way. Look – there's a car over there.'

'It's coming towards us.' Sarah peered over the steering wheel, scouting out the causeway which connected Northumberland with our island destination. 'What's the little hut on stilts halfway across?'

'It's a refuge if you get caught by the tide.'

I had walked across the causeway to Lindisfarne, the Holy Island, a few years ago, with the Scouts. It had been as fine then as it was dour now. I thought it was a marvel of a place. I'd been to Iona – again with the Scouts, as we roamed the Celtic breeding grounds. Iona had a unique tranquillity, as if a magic cloak had been thrown over it and given it a supernatural stillness. Lindisfarne, though still a feature of the barren north which has its almost magnetic pull, threatened to be a livelier place.

But not on the day I persuaded Sarah to go. The causeway was already disappearing under the incoming tide. I had booked a room in a hotel on the island. Quite a chunk of my spending money.

'We'd better move.'

The car jumped into action and went pell-mell into still shallow sea. It was probably a stupid thing to do. The further and faster she drove, the wider Sarah's smile.

'This is great!'

I couldn't agree. I was at the mercy of Sarah's often daredevil driving and the menace of the North Sea determined to claim territory. I felt tense and then, as Sarah laughed at the fun of it all, I tried to make myself relax. The accelerator that challenged the relentless tide and Sarah's determined foot were a reckless combination. She saw that it made me uncomfortable and piled it on.

When we were squarely on the island itself, we stopped to look back. The causeway had disappeared. The hut seemed to be bobbing on the waves like a cork.

'That was great!' she said. 'You didn't like it, did you?'

I refused to answer. She drove sedately to our hotel, small, like everything in the village save the castle and the ruined abbey.

Passing ourselves off as Mr and Mrs Marrs was another hurdle, one that Sarah left to me. As I did it she looked closely at the rack of postcards in the small entrance lobby. The lie was accepted. I'm sure the dull cold weather helped: customers were not plentiful.

It was August, mid-afternoon, heavy-bellied skies threatened. I had loved the island when first I came and I felt no less strongly now. The small castle on its perch at the southern tip. The mighty Bamburgh Castle across the water, marram grass, the bobbing seals and the sound of gulls. I could see the Vikings racing across from the east. Axes raised, war cries chilling the bones of the monks and fisherfolk who made up the small community. Books were stripped of their jewels, the written pages junked by the illiterate Vikings. Precious objects seized and stolen, women carried away to the even further north, pagans crushing a

Christian God who let the Vikings loose — where was He when innocent holy men were slaughtered? The whole picture slapped me in the face. Why did He not preserve those profoundly religious and literate monks, their beacons lighting up the dark age, translating and inscribing the incomparable words of the Gospel in letters of unmatchable beauty — the Lindisfarne Gospels? Monks spending a lifetime on the work.

> I and Pangur Bán, my cat,
> 'Tis a like task we are at:
> Hunting mice is his delight,
> Hunting words I sit all night.
> Better far than praise of men
> 'Tis to sit with book and pen.

That was written by a ninth-century Irish monk. Scholarship, devotion and such skills, I could feel it seep into me from the island itself as continuously as the drizzle which foretold the storm.

The apostolic Celts carried their Christian message from Iona into Northumbria and then across the sea into the Carolingian Empire which transformed much of the known world.

There had been a preservation of high civilisation on this island. It was the chief of several seal-stocked islands, surviving scavenging storms and even the unleashed vandalism of the Norsemen. It scooped my mind away.

'Lynne,' said Sarah, as we set off to walk around the island, 'and Dorothy have gone to Majorca.'

I said nothing.

'Apparently there's a lot going on in Majorca,' Sarah continued grimly, her head bent and butting into the wind. 'They'll come back with tans.'

We were on a hillock. I swept my arm around like my inner anchorite claiming the plain. 'But what about all this?' I said, or rather shouted – the wind was getting up.

'What about it?' said Sarah. 'I'm freezing.' And then she laughed.

'What a dump!' she said. 'And you told me . . .' But the laughter took over.

It rained. It poured. We made straight for the drying room when we cut back to the hotel.

'Dinner at seven,' the lady behind the counter said. 'That gives you about an hour. We have a fire in the sitting room.'

But Sarah was too far gone. She went into laughter more and more. There was nothing I could do but join in. And take a mouthful from the miniature of whisky on the side table, and go to bed.

* * *

Sarah could not be persuaded to go to the annual Wadham College ball.

Michael Wolfers described it to her in embroidered detail. For someone who had never been to such a ball and would never go, it was a masterpiece. He and Sarah had taken to each other and in his popular downstairs room he had tried his considerable best to bring this about. It was as if he were some kind of guidance counsellor with a mission to ensure that Sarah as well as myself got the very best from Oxford.

He described the company who would be at the ball, the rich and handsome and, mostly, eligible young crowd. The bands that would play, floorboards laid on the central lawn for dancing, a constant buffet, indoor and outdoor fireworks, a spectacle of privileged youthful pleasure which, Michael insisted, had to be savoured at least once. 'There'll be dinner parties beforehand, in people's rooms. I expect you'll be invited to some of those.' He smiled confidently at Sarah, whose return smile could not conceal what was plainly a shiver of alarm. 'And it goes on until dawn.' Michael was in full flow. 'Some of them go up the river and filch a punt to see in the sunrise at Magdalen Bridge. It's quite a sight,' he continued, 'the long gowns of the women, flowers in their hair; most of the men in dinner jackets.' He turned to me. 'Hired mostly.' And to Sarah, 'You can hire long dresses too, I'm told.'

'What would I want with hiring a long dress?' she said, rather sharply. 'You'd never know where it's been!'

'But it's part of being at Oxford,' Michael said, 'the Commemoration Ball. Everybody who writes about Oxford includes the Commemoration Ball.'

'I bet you don't.'

Michael looked at Sarah rather waggishly.

'I don't have a partner,' he said. 'And I can't dance.' For reasons which may have been teasing, he went on, 'It's one of the things that people remember about Oxford; it's part of the society of the place. Rather like a debutante's coming-out ball, I imagine.'

'What's that?'

Michael explained.

'That just makes it worse,' she said. 'Pretending to be what you're not.'

'But that's part of being here, isn't it?' Michael leapt on the opportunity. 'We've cast school aside and family aside, we've cast care aside and we can start again. We can pretend to be whatever we want to be.'

'Why should you want to do that?'

'For the fun of it,' Michael replied, firmly.

Sarah turned to me.

'I hope you don't pretend to be what you're not.'

There was a touch of anxiety in her voice.

'Oh,' said Michael, 'he'll never change.'

I felt flattered.

'He doesn't need to,' added Michael.

'I think he's changed a bit already,' said Sarah.

'Some people do. Sometimes all the better for it.'

Sarah looked uncertain. As if she thought, 'where do we go from here?'

'Although,' said Michael, switching track as he liked to do, 'you could argue that Oxford reinforces what we are rather than alters it.'

'What does that mean?'

Michael took care to clarify his words.

'There was a study which showed that most people who came here, men and women, went out fortified in their place in society. The less advantaged undergraduates tended to go into teaching or the lower ranks of the civil service. You could class teaching as a leg up the ladder for some, although it was pointed out that there had been local schoolmasters for many centuries and to be a local teacher or administrator was not considered to be so successful. The very rich, the landed rich and the titled landed rich especially, came and went without any thought or fuss about the future and used it more like a finishing school.' He had worked it through. He went on, 'The rest are divided into the contented spear carriers and the outsiders. Those who were fully-fledged outsiders, like myself, or those who found they could develop talents at university in ways not available at their unfashionable public schools – like the one I went to – or increasingly they came from grammar schools, and veered towards the edgy or the non-institutional – actors, journalists, arty types, oddballs, sometimes successful, sometimes interesting failures. Oxford was set up to train clerics in theology, scholars in classics and turn out lawyers.' He smiled, that wide sweet sensuous smile. 'It still does. That's why I aim to be a lawyer!'

'You didn't mention women.'

'True, Sarah, true and reprehensible, but they will have their day. The suffragettes took their time. I'm sure they will be too clever to keep out.'

'You make it sound rather rigid,' I said. 'I haven't found that.'

'There are exceptions,' said Michael, 'but I suspect that the university is an agent for consolidation rather than innovation. What we need is a revolution, yet most of us will be lassoed into the Establishment.'

'Have you written about that?'

'I will. It's on the way,' said Michael, thoughtfully, 'but I'm not as assiduous as you. And besides, I prefer being an outsider to being a participant. I feel much more secure that way.'

* * *

Sarah and I had quarrelled. We had parted twice over the years but soon got back together. The quality of this silence between us as we walked into the city to find a cheap restaurant was of a different character.

We sat at a corner table, ordered in silence, lit up in silence, waited for the other to begin. I cracked first.

'He's very clever,' I said.

Sarah nodded, paused.

'So many of your friends are clever.'

'So are you,' I said.

That was a mistake.

'Don't be daft.'

'Why don't you believe me?'

She shook her head.

I went on, 'Clever isn't just passing exams. Shakespeare didn't pass any exams. Clever's something you're born with.'

Sarah let it drop.

Chicken, roast potatoes, vegetables. A glass of white wine for Sarah, beer for me. An unusually silent supper.

'What is it?'

Sarah shook her head. She pushed aside a half-eaten meal and said quietly, 'I keep thinking of the long dresses and the dinner parties. It's not for me. It never will be. It's another world.'

'It needn't be.'

'But it could be yours, couldn't it? Maybe you would want it to be. I think it's where you're going. Dinner parties! Long dresses! I'd be lost.'

'I'm sure you could manage.'

'I don't want to manage.'

'Give it time.'

'Why?'

'Well. Forget it. Who cares?'

'I think that you do. And your friends. Ulick and Robert and Alan and Michael as well for all I know.'

'I can't see them bothering.'

'I can. If they had to. And you would. If you had to.'

'But not you?'

She spoke more slowly than usual. She was always measured but now it was as if every word had to be weighed.

'I don't think so,' she said in a low voice so that no one but me could possibly hear her. She took her time. 'Because I don't want to. I don't want to be like that.'

She smiled, a strained smile, and shook her head.

'Never mind,' she said. Those two words passed the problem from her on to me.

'But we're all right, aren't we?'

She nodded.

'We are,' she said. 'We are.' She took a sip of the wine.

Chapter Twenty-one

We were in bed. A single bed. In a room without heating and usually that would have been part of the fun. Warming up. Sarah was not fully undressed. We usually slept naked. Our bodies locking and unlocking without impediment. It had not been a happy day. I found it difficult to pinpoint the cause of our dark mood or rather Sarah's mood. Something festered. It had been building up and to every question of 'Are you all right?' came 'Fine, thank you.' Or 'Is there anything I can do?' 'Nothing.'

The Oxford Experience had something to do with it, I was sure of that – but what? There had not been a significant incident which might have seeded this switch. We had left Oxford behind and come to Bath for a couple of days. We'd found a cheap enough bed and breakfast place clumsily converted out of stables. Street light came in through the ill-fitting curtains and I could see that her eyes were closed, hear that her breathing was regular, sense from her immobility that she did not want to be disturbed. I lay flat on my back, wide-eyed, feeling that in my head was a hornet's nest. There was a smell which reminded me of the barn in Oulton. I looked at her as if watching over her. She looked so lovely.

Abruptly she sat up.

'This is no good.'

'It was all that was left.' We had, with difficulty, found a place in Bath which was affordable but admittedly grim.

'I'm not talking about the room.' She reached out to the small table on her side of the bed, flicked on the side light, took a cigarette, offered one to me. She pulled her knees towards her.

'What's the matter?'

She took a deep draw on the cigarette.

'I don't know how to say it.'

Her words were alien to the way we talked to each other.

'To say what?'

She shook her head, drew more deeply on the cigarette and looked away.

'I don't know how to say it,' she repeated. Her voice sounded uncharacteristically fragile.

Sarah took a deep breath, stubbed out the cigarette, turned to face the shadowy figure next to her and said, very quietly, 'I don't think we should go on.'

She got out of bed. Put on her dressing gown, went across to the window and drew the curtains. It had the beginnings of a fine dawn. She lit a fresh cigarette.

Thinking back, I have little detailed memory of my initial reaction. I assume it was shock and alarm. We had fallen out before – but this from the beginning was on a different plane. I remember the tone, the emphasis and context of her words and the way I received them. She had settled herself for an end.

It was over.

How could it be?

It was over.

She turned away. It was a gentle move but emphatic. She just turned away. I moved forward and held out my arms to hold her but she shook her head slightly and inched further away.

How could this be happening? After more than three years, after so much life together. So many promises . . . ?

'I'll make us a cup of coffee,' she said. And I sat on the edge of the bed and watched Sarah make two cups of Nescafé. Nothing was said until she came and sat beside me. The coffee was scalding.

'I can't believe it,' I said.

She nodded.

'It's been coming on for some time.'

'What's been coming on?'

'This.'

I had been frozen out.

'Can't we talk about it?'

'What is there to talk about?' Sarah spoke that simple sentence emphatically, as if she had rehearsed.

'Not long ago we were ready to get married.'

'Just as well we didn't.'

That was a stab.

'Things can't change just like that. There must be a reason.'

Sarah put the cup of coffee on the floor.

'It has been building up,' she said. 'I'll admit that.'

'I didn't notice.'

Sarah laughed.

'I took good care you didn't notice.'

There was a silence through which I could not navigate.

'Was it Oxford?'

Sarah nodded.

'I thought you liked the people.'

'I did. I do! Robert and Ulick and Alan and Michael. They seemed to know everything and you couldn't meet kinder people. I kept thinking weren't you lucky to have such friends. And they were very nice to me.'

The pause lengthened.

'If it was anybody' – Sarah spoke slowly and deliberately, perhaps unconsciously exposing the flatness of her accent – 'it was the girls, the women. I just felt I was so out of place. They talked so – not poshly, but so differently from me – and the way they seemed to have an opinion about everything made me feel ignorant. And those would be the people you would associate with after Oxford, I knew that. I would be lost. I know I would. And the dresses – not just what they wore that time we went to the theatre and I was the only one who dressed like me. It was all flowing skirts and flowery dresses you'd have liked me to wear for the Ball. But I could never wear one of those. For one thing I'm not tall enough, but I wouldn't *want* to either, that's what I'm trying to say, I wouldn't *want* to. And then there were these dinner parties people kept talking about. What do I want with dinner parties? And . . . It's just the way of life, as they anticipate it, as *you* anticipate it – how could it ever be mine? And anyway I don't want it to be mine. You could, you could get used to it, I'll bet on that. But I wouldn't and I couldn't and, I'm sorry . . .' Suddenly there were tears. 'I *can't*. I just can't.'

* * *

It is difficult to describe my reaction at the time. It has not got easier. I don't want to use words like 'struck dumb' or 'distraught'. From sixty years' distance such terms still seem too dramatic. We were young after all and those decades have passed by, though unburied, and I want to understand for myself the effect it had on my life.

A couple of her London friends she worked with at the bank used to tease her by saying that she would soon get bored with me. She told them about art galleries and museums and foreign films with me endlessly explaining and trying to force on her an education she found that she resisted. Or perhaps it was my insistence *itself* that disturbed her. Was she forever to be a pupil? Just as when first we went into the Lake District together, until she said I was spoiling it for her by acting like a tour guide. She wanted to see it and value it for herself. I stopped and she said it got better. I now made the effort not to be oppressive in London.

But I had fallen into the same habit when we went to the Tate or the National Gallery – and I especially remember when I was punishingly thorough about one of the Rembrandt self-portraits. He was already my favourite painter but in this particular self-portrait you saw an old man, baggily breasted, dressed like an old woman. When you looked closely you saw that one eye was dead, no light, no life, and the other shone, saw everything, was life itself. The painting had fascinated me and I tried to pass that on to Sarah and she got it. For the first time, she was as absorbed as I was. What I did not confess was that the Rembrandt obsessive self-portraits fortified what I was beginning to try in my writing . . . a cat may look at a queen . . . and slowly it dawned on me that I could be my subject – no shame or weakness in that. And who would read or judge it anyway?

She was more at home at the Tate, with the Turner landscapes. She saw them as part of her Cumbrian life. Away from her family and her local friends who might well have reacted with an amiable shrug, she began to try to take on the gallery life. 'Art and English were the only subjects I liked at school,' she said at that time. 'Especially art. Miss Robert, the art teacher, said I should go on with it.'

'Why didn't you?'

'I'd had enough of school.'

Over the next few weeks I tried to work out why this break-up had happened. It was my fault. Nothing would budge that. But it was always the same question. Why and how had the two of us split so – to me – unexpectedly, out of nowhere, when we had been together so closely for so long?

She had 'gone off' me. Whatever those words meant, I thought that they applied here. I realised that she had signalled this for some time but the message had failed to reach me. Now it did. Whatever had been between us had drained away. Oxford had been a step too far.

Why? Was her explanation about the girls at Oxford and the future it seemed to demand the whole explanation? I'm sure I could have given up Oxford. But she barred that. Oxford was only the trigger, I thought: the reason was deeper. She'd had enough in a way that defied simple explanations.

When I asked her directly, her answers were as much to protect me as to explain us. She had known only one 'boyfriend' before me and that hadn't mattered. I think it meant she was tired of who I was, my habits dulled through repetition, or just dull anyway. What I could have thought of as exciting teenage years were not enriched by our fidelity. She wanted more fun. She wanted to explore; she wanted different experiences. Was that it? Did she feel trapped? Had too little happened?

Why did I not fight back? Why did I not plague her with renewed proposals, see it as a passing stage, as just one of those things? Did I take her words so seriously that I lost words of my own?

It was not words that wounded. It was the flinching away from me, not dramatic but noticeable. As if my touch or our touching would prolong and be an unwelcome reminder of a passion now dying. It said I want us to be separate; separate, her gestures and her body said. She went back to Wigton alone.

When, after some days, I fully realised what had happened, I felt the pain of loss. When I turned to her in the bed, she was not there. Life without her made me feel that I wanted to fend off all contact with everyone. I was becoming enfeebled. At the core of the matter, I was spiralling slowly into isolation. However much I thought we were just two young people breaking up, it wasn't part of any pattern I could accept. It would not blow away in the wind. Her decisive rejection killed off what had been central to my life.

How to go on without her? It did not bear thinking about. I felt a cold slab in my mind. What would happen next? So much that was the best in my life had happened with Sarah. Risks, growth, sex, fun, a way of looking at the world and sizing it up, the sense of a future. Now I felt imprisoned and alone in myself. Not unlike the time of the breakdown years before. A sense of drifting away from all that mattered. Suddenly a trapdoor had opened and I fell. Kept falling.

What was I going to do without her? Juvenile as that question might seem; weak as it could be described, that was the heart of it. What would I do without her?

I phoned. Her father answered. 'She isn't here,' he said, and for such a tough man, the voice was uncharacteristically gentle. I took it to mean that she wanted no contact.

I was black-minded and sorry for myself. I had thoughts way beyond previous teenage unhappiness. But there it was. You can be the most ordinary man but you can suffer from the deep root rejection of a great love, as if you had fallen into an abyss. 'No worst, there is none.' It can seem foolish now, but it happened and it happens everywhere and every day. My body, the thing I was, that makes me live, was simply dead. I humped it around, longing, even praying – though I felt hypocritical about that – to get rid of this me, this carcase of misery that was wearing away my life. However self-indulgent and excessive it seems now, that was what was happening then – a daily struggle, it seemed, against an implacable, oppressive, empty future.

Worst of all, where was she? Was she with someone else?

Why were we no longer together? Who was there to turn to? Share with? Be alive with?

I went to Reading for a few days but the rawness I felt was so transparent, especially to my mother, that I phoned Wadham – it was the beginning of January – and I asked if I could rent a room in College until the next term began.

I had fallen behind with work and as once before, at school, when I had been totally out of joint, work, over-intensive, mind-exhausting work, had seen me through. Holed up alone, with books, might do it again. There was no other way I could think of.

None of my friends were staying in College for the vacation. There was peace in that, space and time to cope and attempt to reset my life. Sorry about the exaggerated phrasing but the truth was I held on, that was all. That was the best I could do.

Part Two

Chapter Twenty-two

Years later we met and talked about it, when life had moved on for each of us, when we began what would be a lifelong friendship, when I began to phone Sarah regularly, and we talked about the break-up.

It was strange to think of loneliness, she said, of that time when she was surrounded by work friends during the day and by her oldest village friends in the evenings. But she too had this loneliness which she had never felt before. It crept into her mind; she could feel the cold grip of it, she said, and it seemed to squat there. She had not realised how much she had given and taken from us. The feeling of loss deepened. She had not anticipated that. She had thought that separation would somehow be self-healing. That a new state would be easy to assume, not a trial. Not a trial every morning, every night, hemmed in by what was no longer available.

And yet she could not give in, she said. It had meant too much to leave, to be able to upturn her feelings, feelings that had festered and she had fostered for so long. The more she thought about it the harder it got. And then she met Juan . . .

* * *

For me too in the beginning it was strange, almost weird, being alone. For more than three years we had been a pair.

Whenever I turned around – she had been there. Going out meant going out with Sarah, meeting up with people meant that the two of us would meet up with people. Walking down the street was never aimless because later that day I would phone, see, go out with Sarah. I knew it was fruitless thinking along these lines. Surely the manly thing was to take it on the chin and move on. To grin and bear it. Or pretend it did not matter. But it did. Every day. I tried to lift myself out of it by insulting myself: feeble was the kindest word I came up with.

It was as if a twin from the past was always alongside me. She was there like a reflection in a mirror or a shadow that would always follow me or I would follow her.

I am sure that this is a common feeling – the effect of such sudden emotional loss. Pop songs are full of heartache; the best songs understand the power of it. I could understand why poetic lovers had 'pined away': pining away is what happens; the world loses its savour and the smallest matters call for exhausting effort. There's a wasting tiredness. There was an intensifying emptiness all the more painful because it was unspoken. What could I say? Who could I talk to? It was a sickness.

* * *

My mother and I visited my father's grave, soon after his burial. Both of us stood immobile and in silence for some time, and then my mother broke away, I should write 'wrenched' herself away, and in a voice of quiet torment she said, 'I miss him terribly.' She stumbled along the narrow cemetery path and I paused before following her. Who could replace him? I understood why love could cause people to fade away.

I had to learn to be alone. I had to accept it. 'It's all over.' Four syllables said it. It was finished. What next? What now? There was this draining feeling of being trapped in myself, shuttered in; the loss and the pain dominated my feelings.

That was the case.

* * *

When I went back to Oxford for the rest of the Christmas vacation I saw it as a bolthole. At first I thought that the only course to take was to go back immediately to Wigton and face Sarah and not let it go by way of a letter. Sarah's letters were few, short, polite, full stop. Firm. I saw no way through. She could be inside my mind and outside, at the end of a pen, at the same time. Inventing what she might be doing was a substitute for feeling, as the heavy reading had been at school.

The College let me hire a room in the back quad near the new library. There was breakfast – no other meals – for the few of us who had taken advantage of the College's vacation hospitality.

At first I merely went through the motions. Took books off the shelves, made notes, filed them. I had let work slip while with Sarah and it was a challenge to myself to dig in, like old times, to push myself, like old times, to challenge the strain. Wadham had not got a First in history recently and scholarship men were supposed to change that. One of my regular tutors said they had 'hopes'. As before, concentration on academic work was a way to push out other preoccupations. But where once it had been exhilarating, now it was exhausting. Sarah hovered on my shoulder, circled in my thoughts, interfering with the lists of history. Yet now and then I could feel I was getting there as the monastic life took grip. I began to build a routine . . .

* * *

The routine, the new life, was broken by a wave across Broad Street outside Balliol College from a man who was also vacationing in our College. I knew him only slightly. Alistair Tod, son of an admiral. I responded to his wave by walking across to the College where he had stopped and waited, clearly happy for company.

He was heading for a party in the village of Shillingford, a few miles away, given by arts students from Ruskin College. He was sure I'd be welcome. All that I needed was to take a bottle of wine, any wine would do.

The party was given by two American art students who shared the house. The guests – save for Alistair and myself – were all from the Ruskin School of Art, which was housed inside the Ashmolean Museum. There was elementary food on a long trestle table, beer and wine on a shorter table, low jazz and people sitting on the floor in an attractive dusky light, a pleasant hubbub.

Elisabeth – Lisa – appeared to be isolated. She also seemed somehow sufficient to herself. There was a gap on the floor beside her and I took it. Asked her if she wanted a drink. Happily heaved up to fetch a white wine and returned with relief. My spot had not been appropriated.

I can't remember anything that we talked about. Most likely we exchanged some basic information – you French, me English, you art student, me history undergraduate and suchlike pearls. Neither of us seemed full of the Christmas spirit. Both rather depressed, which brought us together.

We had found a site – on the floor. We showed no inclination to move away and join one of the groups of her fellow students.

Lisa was not made for small talk; I had the impression on that first evening that she was scarcely present, her conversation was so low on energy and substance. In the arty candle glow it was difficult to see nuanced moods but clear that the overwhelming mood was sadness. She looked rather too old to be a student. Her slightly long face was finely shaped, slim body, grey eyes, a mouth quick to offer a glancing smile, long hair loosely, carelessly, tied. Nothing about her appearance was studied or set up for show. Nor was the dress she wore. Her whole appearance said there were better ways to spend your time than to make yourself look sexy or chic. We were ignored even though we were in the middle of the floor.

When I remember that first encounter I keep returning to the sadness. She seemed enwrapped in it even though she was surrounded by students. Her engagement with me was for good manners and the useful distraction of new company. Or was it the sadness I myself had which brought out a matching response, a mating call in its way? The semi-darkness of the room and her mood began to work like a mutual gentle hypnosis. Without effort she spoke in swift cultivated English, only the scarcest trace of an accent, a willingness to stay beside me if that were required but to stay anyway because movement meant change which carried the risk of encounters she might not want. I was good enough for the moment. Or so I assumed. We were given a lift back to Oxford and I took note of her address. By then I had learned that she lived with a philosopher and his family as an au pair but with light duties. She had a small, regular income from France where her father, she told me, was a teacher who lived in Paris.

The information I offered was that I was from the north, in my final year and on my own.

Chapter Twenty-three

Lisa was frugal about autobiographical information. As time went by she preferred to listen to me on my background. At times I felt like a member of a rather primitive tribe, but for the most part she somehow steered the conversation on to more general levels, skirmishing with ideas rather than gossiping or swapping Oxford stories.

The house she lived in was a tall, rather battered Georgian terraced townhouse on four floors near the centre of the city. Elegance and bookishness were the key. High ceilings, finely proportioned rooms, built for style and bookshelves, yet holding on to family comforts. Lisa lived in a small bed-sitter at the top of three flights of stairs, overlooking rooftops; a bit like a garret in Paris, she said, where she had been brought up.

Drawn in by a relentlessly encroaching loneliness, I called on her a few days after the party. The boy who opened the door confidently ushered me up the stairs, calling out Lisa's name to prepare her.

It was the first occasion on which I had spent time in a house and with the family of an Oxford don. A cup of tea here, a sherry there, geniality everywhere. From the day I went around I found an unfussy welcome, good manners and a scholarly family intelligence foreign to my experience. There was a sophisticated and easy invitation from the boy to take me to 'the top of the stairs'.

There was something about the house that made it the most attractive home I'd ever encountered outside Wigton. Perhaps it was the pervasiveness of the good manners. And there was a gracefulness combined with a studious ease, a piano in the front room – two of the children played – well-worn rugs, pictures, prints, a few photographs, but most of all books. Books which were there not to furnish the room but as evidence of what mattered. Books read or waiting their turn. Tidily arranged, mostly scuffed from use, not so much part of the furniture as the furniture itself. Perhaps this was the typical don's lair. I liked everything about it. The basic order, the superficial carelessness, the way the furniture was for ease and not for comment, unpretentious yet impressive, plain living and high thinking, as if every sentence spoken had been rehearsed and polished.

The philosopher, Professor Peter Strawson, was lean, handsome, impeccably polite. His wife Ann, every bit as attractive, quick and clever, seemingly inexhaustible, perhaps from the work she and a friend put in at their allotment. They were the flow of the place. They seemed to glide through it. The four children, young at that time, as free as could be but not butting in. Perhaps the ample space did that, or more likely the atmosphere, dispensed by Peter and Ann. It was a place which quietly and persistently valued intellect.

So this was how Oxford kept and bred its tutors! They would pass on this civilised world to their children and their pupils, creating a stream of learning. There was an unfaltering respect for truths gained through scholarship as carefully as in previous times and in places not unlike Oxford today. At that time the monks had prayed and worked looking for the sources of spiritual conviction. Now the creed was largely secular scholarship. But the pursuit was not too dissimilar.

What most impressed me was the precision of vocabulary between Peter and Ann even over the most mundane matters. They were the same age. Ann's degree, a First, was superior to that of Peter. Both came from unpretentious middle-class families, but their habit or determination to allot the exact weight to every sentence, phrase and word gave to their conversation the flavour of a two-way seminar, even a play. Always seeking out the perfect sentence.

At times I felt I was an audience – not that there was the slightest show in what they did – but it deserved an audience. With Peter it was a habit grown out of his philosophical research, his academic work, a fusion forever to be set in perfect prose. Ann's contribution could appear more natural, but the more I heard the more it resembled Peter's speech, another branch on the same tree. It was effortlessly serious, unpompous and, in my experience, unique.

The house of Peter and Ann and their family had as much effect on me as all the advantages of College life. It was here, I believed, in such a home, that Oxford held its finest treasure. Or so I thought then, just emerging from my teens. And so I think now halfway through my ninth decade.

Lisa had landed here by accident, by luck. That first night, she called down and I went up the stairs, and more stairs, and into the first artist's studio I had ever entered and into a life I could never have dreamt of.

* * *

I still sent short, urgent messages to Sarah. She replied in a steady negative. I could not accept that it had happened, although clearly it had and it was continuing to happen with no sign of reconciliation on Sarah's part.

Work was an important distraction but in the early days after we split up it did not last long enough or bite in deeply enough. Instead of being absorbed in it for its own sake, which had once created a world proofed against outside interventions, it came up against the force of a three-year passion. I was as abandoned as a whelp in the woods.

Sarah blocked entry to the past. Perhaps I should have raced to Cumbria and talked her out of it? But her short notes were firm. I should have . . . I could have . . . time would bring us together again . . . But her notes were far from the lament of an unhappy woman. Our course was run. How could I express to her how deeply she was lodged inside me when her constant signals were – over, end and out . . .

So for those Christmas festival days in Oxford I walked around as a wounded thing, sorry for myself.

Until I met Lisa.

There was a great deal Lisa withheld. The few facts came out reluctantly, heavily edited. The one central matter a friend of hers, also at the party, alluded to was that Lisa was depressed because she had just broken up with her American boyfriend – who had also been at Ruskin College. A few weeks later, when Lisa and I had begun to see each other regularly, the friend passed the information on to me. They had been very close – that was stressed – but suddenly an American academic post called and he was off. Lisa was abandoned.

We were, then, in some measure, two of a kind. That can repel as well as attract but here, by small footsteps, it began to attract. Lisa's personality was like that of no one I had ever met. There was pain in her eyes which I recognised, a pain, as time went on, which could carry flashes of humour, dry, witty, or relax into the beginnings of affection. Neither of us was interested in anyone else after that first meeting on the floor in Shillingford and so it continued for some time. Both of us wanted to repair what had seemed irreparable damage. Chastely we explored each other's foreign and scarcely comprehensible backgrounds.

She saw me in her French hierarchy as a peasant. Yet I sensed that I was also someone whose enthusiasm could sweep away her mourning and challenge her lethargy. For instance, she had failed a set of exams at Ruskin College twice. She stayed on at the College because her father's allowance paid her modest fees and one of her teachers believed in the talent although he could do nothing to help her summon her energy to pass the examination paper. The Art School was an atmosphere in which she was comfortable. Academic Oxford and the academic Strawson household had enough affinity with her own background – the particulars of which she admitted very gradually. All I knew at that time for sure was that she was extraordinarily clever, complex, unexpected, and appeared not to be reluctant for us to be together. I could think of it as a version of *The Princess and the Pauper*. There seemed to be no magic to resolve it happily ever after. Save that it appeared to work for the moment and the moments began to add up. Perhaps our separate losses as outsiders were somehow transformed into a gain. We were both losers with, it seemed, nowhere else to go. And no will to go anywhere else. We were on the bottom rung of the ladder of courting, mating, coupling with little more to lose. What else could we do? Neither of us had the advantage. We had an equality of uncertainty and unhappiness.

* * *

Lisa. I have written about Lisa before in *Remember Me* . . . But she has to be part of these final Oxford months. She defined them for me, transformed and directed them in a unique way.

We began what became our 'affair' a few weeks after we had come back from Shillingford. For me it was a plunge through ice.

Although I had a berth in the College, I began to use Lisa's room more frequently. There were encounters on the stairs with the family, a smile, a polite greeting, and I passed by. It was frictionless.

The company was so stylish. So this was what life could be like! My association was cemented when the adults, Peter and Ann, accepted a trip to an American university for a fortnight and asked Lisa and myself if we would look after the house and the children. Lisa saw it as an adventure. I was flattered.

The children were back at school which took care of much of the day when I could get on with my work and Lisa concentrate on hers.

It was inexplicable to me she had twice failed those written examinations at the Art School. But her failure could have been calculated. It ensured that she could stay on for another year as a fee-paying student. Which is what she wanted. It was a strategy. That must have been the reason. She spoke of her home life in France in very little detail or affection. Where was she to go if she left the Ruskin? If she left Oxford? I did not realise how safe she saw that her English life was and yet how fragile. Only in occasional sentences or hurt outbursts of her life in France did I begin to build up a picture of who she was. Her life story came in brief disclosures, linked by that thrum of melancholy that seemed to permeate her in our early days. The times of animated debates and clever insights were occasional lights along a dark road. But between them, the teachers and pupils at the School of Art and the liberal, sometimes gossipy, almost racy style of the Strawsons' house were gradually healing the wounds of her childhood.

I was not able to put the following facts in an order until much later.

She was twenty-five; I was twenty-one. She was taking on the after-effects of an affair with an American artist who had been at the Ruskin with her. She never mentioned this until, a while after we had met, she announced that he was coming back to Oxford and he had asked her to meet him. By this time we were lovers and practically inseparable. I watched with jealousy the way in which she dressed and made herself ready for this encounter. She told me where they would meet, in the courtyard of a pub near Wadham. She looked wonderful, expectant, unbearable. After an hour I could stand it no longer, sought out the pub, joined them for drinks, uninvited, and stuck it out until he left.

I never saw him again. He wrote to Lisa when he was back in the States, asking her to join him. From his letters, as far as I could tell – using Warden Bowra's favourite term of dismissal – he was 'a shit'.

I had never met anyone remotely like Lisa. There was not only the foreignness in birth but also in her manner, her intellect, differences that could make her seem inaccessible. Above all there was that melancholy, present even when she laughed, an impenetrable cloak that cut her off, moated her, I thought. I recognised myself there: it was an atmosphere I wanted to dispel.

It seemed from the beginning that she was calling out for help but the cry, so quiet, scarcely reached me. More than anything, there was her complexity which had a strong sense of itself. The nearer you got to her the more entangled it became. She analysed me as we went along. I was unused to this and uneasy about it. She always outboxed me, telling me who I was and what I thought. I had little defence. She enjoyed reconstructing me.

To record her life in a neat biography would be to misrepresent both of us. Caution ran parallel with the impulse to know. What I got to understand about her over those first months came slowly, in fragments, rarely followed through, stopped as abruptly as if shame, or diffidence, regret, or more likely anger, got in the way of her story.

Her mother had died a few months after she was born. Her mother had been a distinguished scientist, like her father, and worked alongside him on research into the adrenalin gland. I understood they were recommended for a Nobel Prize. At his wife's death he, Lisa emphasised, was distraught and handed her over (this information came later from friends of her mother) to an uncaring and – Lisa used the word – 'cruel' woman who tricked her studious father into believing she was a good foster mother. The experience, these friends of Lisa's mother told me, marred her for life.

Another World

Her father married again, a professional musician from Norway with whom he had four children. Lisa believed that they soaked up all the maternal affection available, leaving Lisa to be brought up like an orphan. This brief summary does no justice to her emotional tension and occasional fury. That she had been given a mean Christmas present, rebuffed, overlooked repeatedly: it was a catalogue of petty exclusions and persecution. It had not helped that her father's second wife was forever being compared to her disadvantage to the brilliant first wife, Lisa's mother.

Lisa had failed her baccalaureate to her own shame and her father's open disappointment. The subsequent distress led to what almost amounted to ostracism from her family which took her to the south of France near Montpellier, where she stayed with an old friend and colleague of her father – another scientist – and his kindly wife, herself childless. They saw Lisa through for two years and seemed to have stabilised her. In that time she went to the art school in Montpellier and also studied English . . .

It is unclear what happened next save that her father, on a visit to Oxford, mentioned his daughter's interest in painting and, without consulting her, at his wife's suggestion thought it would be helpful were she to be allowed to apply for the Ruskin School of Art. She did and got in, helping to pay her way by taking on au pair work, first with a history don and his unsympathetic family and then, through one of the lifelines that tied the university's teachers together, in the house of Peter and Ann Strawson which, she would say, was 'the first real home I ever had'.

Her father, whom she had told me was a teacher, turned out to be one of the few men in French academic history to be simultaneously head of the College de France and the Sorbonne, in which he lived in a large flat. Her birth mother was a viscountess. The title went down the female line but Lisa was enraged were anyone to mention that. I had no idea how to cope with any of this. But there was no need. We wouldn't talk about it. After she went to Oxford her stepmother was pleased that she was not in France – they had tormented each other enough. She announced to her friends that an English Education would be good for her and calm her down. Her stepmother was right. Oxford's academic air and easy student life, especially in the Ruskin, gave her a niche, let her grow in confidence and to some extent build a nest.

What I have written has been stitched together from scraps. The chief point was that in Oxford there was a cessation of two matters. The first was the pain of being an outsider in her own family which her time in England partially solved as her life in Paris could not. Then, as importantly, her mind found spaces of peace in reading and writing poetry in English. Finally there were her bold paintings.

The breezy arty student life, the tolerance, the broken love affairs, the friendships and the threats from her past were now over the sea. But as her refusal to pass exams showed, there was a survivalist instinct to stay where she was. Her attic in Banbury Road within the house was not so much her refuge as her fortress. It stabilised her. But nothing alleviated the fact that for the second time, she had been abandoned. I was out of my depth. Too much was too difficult to understand at that time let alone absorb. Sometimes it seemed that we were strangers to each other and yet, through need and circumstances, we drew closer together.

* * *

I may have emphasised Lisa's melancholy too strongly. There was a joy which burst out and could be glowing with life. The problem is that I see her from several different angles and in different moods as I write this. Although I try hard to keep to the past, keep to that time in Oxford when we were young, it is sometimes the later days, the end days, that seize attention and command memory.

As the weeks went on I began to see her through a steadier lens: her eyes were grey to pale blue and could flick from sad to gay in a moment. These moments became more frequent. Were they, as is claimed, the windows to the soul? In which case Lisa's soul was pure. Even so, I can still puzzle that the emptiness after the separation from Sarah was filled so soon by Lisa. Yet it did not make me doubt how much I had loved Sarah. Our children are friends. My daughter Marie-Elsa and Sarah's daughter Maria are close. Maria is a fully committed biker and a much sought-after carer. Marie-Elsa is a priest and a writer.

Lisa and I slipped into bed together without the excruciating testing time and obstacle course which was the Wigton custom. One night, late, cold, tired, instead of making for my new digs, we just went into bed and afterwards I fell asleep and stayed there. This again was not remarked on by the Strawson household. Perhaps this meant that it was a common occurrence, or they decided it was none of their business. After all, her attic flat was her domain. I could not believe it was common practice. Yet perhaps it was what artists and philosophers did, wasn't it? Iris Murdoch was a friend of Peter and Ann and, it seemed, embraced sexual pluralism. And it was what some of the dons did. They were bohemians; they did not follow normal patterns. Lisa's character was in her eyes. Her eyes were messengers, I thought; despite all her torments, she was still finding joy in life.

* * *

By this time a new term had started. For this our last year the undergraduates had to find digs in the city. There were licensed landladies. Ulick and I shared part of the upstairs of a semi-detached house in Marston, a village about a mile from the centre of Oxford, past Magdalen College grounds, where, with luck, as we walked back we would get a glimpse of the College's herd of deer. Then over the bridge with its famous tower and into the acreage of the non-academic part of the city.

It was a bus ride or, more often, an unexciting morning and evening walk. Our landlady, Mrs Prior, also worked in the College. She was strict. She provided breakfast at 8.00 a.m. Mr Prior, rather understandably we thought, spent a considerable amount of his free time in his garden shed where, Mrs Prior told us, he liked to 'make things for the house'.

As the winter struggled on, I began to stay with Lisa more frequently. I was putting in the hours now for the Finals which were only a few months away. Marston seemed an unnecessary haul at the end of a day in the library . . .

When I was summoned to the rooms of Wadham's Moral Tutor I had no idea what was in store. He was a New

Zealander, exceptionally easy-going. But not on this particular morning at 10.30 a.m.

'We've had a complaint about you.'

He knew the remark would puzzle me and let it simmer for a few moments. 'From Mrs Prior.'

No reaction. I paid the rent; I was quite tidy around the place; I was mostly back before 11 p.m., which was the rule. But for Mrs Prior 'mostly' was not enough.

'Mrs Prior is one of our most valued landladies. *And* she lends a hand in the dining hall when requested. She is upset. She doesn't know where you are.'

The only answer was the truth but I could sense that wasn't going to take me very far. When in doubt, say nowt.

'It's of no consequence to me where you are on your absent nights. But it is of great consequence that Mrs Prior is not upset. She is an experienced employee. She has complained that your behaviour gives her Restless Nights, lying awake, waiting for you to come in and when you don't, with no forewarning, she feels that she has let us all down. She sees you as her responsibility. Her health, she says, is under strain.'

'I hadn't realised. I'm sorry but—'

'But no buts. You're here to work, not to be Jack the Lad. Fifteen pounds fine, payable by tomorrow. Any further breaches will be taken more seriously. You could be sent down. Why don't you say you're visiting a relative or some such – anything will do – but not this blatant truancy.'

'Truancy?'

'That's what I'm calling it. Get your love life under control.' He paused. 'I think that's all.'

He turned away, possibly to conceal a smile. My court martial was over.

Restless Nights.

* * *

For supper Lisa and I would go to a small cafe, meagrely supported, hope for the corner table and have the 'choice of the day' which was also the least expensive. I had been thrifty and enjoyed the gesture of paying the bill. Afterwards we would go back to her flat, and we would either part on the doorstep of the house and I would set off on the trek to Marston or we would go up to Lisa's room for the night. Now and then I invented trips to my parents in Reading and now and then Mrs Prior allowed herself to be convinced.

We talked about each other. Lisa carefully shielded and selected what she said; I dipped my recollections with an accuracy which, I could see, made me seem as exotic to her as she was to me. Lisa's reticence came from a tight grip on the privacy she saw as essential. She considered her exalted pedigree to be an obstacle. My reactions were sometimes beefed up because I could sense that the contrast entertained her. I was something of an anthropological study.

It seemed that we had very little in common, yet we shared hours of talk. She had a mind that could tug out every last gram of a discussion and phrase it in terms closer than I had ever come across.

Her reading was all but exclusively in French, mine in English. She loved chansons, Édith Piaf, Charles Aznavour, Jacques Brel, Charles Trenet . . . I had never heard of them. Her introduction to my interest in the eruption of British and American pop music was just as foreign to her: rock'n'roll was my generation's background music; Lisa had little time for it and that 'little' was out of politeness. She spoke fluent English well enough to write poetry and compose the essays she at last got round to writing. My French was 'kitchen French' at best, fifth form stuff.

A couple of months after we met, Michael negotiated an occasional column on art history in *Cherwell* for her. The way that small communities – like universities – work meant that soon enough she was quite well known. She studied the paintings and drawings in the Museum. She drew on its archives of Renaissance drawings. We led a life together. She sipped white wine. I drank beer. I loved tramping around the parks and the meadows. She complimented me on my peasant sturdiness but as often as not was happy for me to go alone.

Soon it was obvious how much I thought of her and how strongly though warily that was reciprocated. I was willing to be drawn into her web. There was often a particular smile, apparently amused at my extremes of enthusiasm. When I picked that up I didn't object. There was too much that was good to fret. Neither of us sensed any danger. Soon we were close friends as well as lovers, well content in each other's exclusive company, seeking each other out.

Yet the gap was wide. French aristocracy, academic brilliance in a train of generations of scholarly grandeur. Northern English working class, neither of my parents staying on at school after the age of fourteen. Able to meet on what seemed the equal terms of Oxford. How did that happen? The caste system appeared to be suspended for the specialised purpose of the university. Most of us didn't care, or deliberately failed to bow to the obvious distinctions. If anything we found them putty medals.

Yet when I was there, the Bullingdon Club – with its entitled or faux-rich members, with its self-congratulatory appalling rudeness and snob-fuelled behaviour – was still considered a breeding ground for political eminence. It was to give us two of our worst prime ministers, who went on to become spivs. The Club thought it great fun to smash up a restaurant, thinking that a few fivers would make things okay with the serfs. They didn't: they merely added to the casually nasty snobbery. England could still be a mediaeval collection of tribes, largely undisturbed for centuries with its Norman pyramid of privilege and wealth. This was a current which ran under culture, land rights, clubs. Some of it was harmless, some was entertaining, but its politics of exclusion could mangle those involved and stunt them if unchallenged.

In those university days you could lead the lives you wanted to lead. With luck, pave your own path. We proceeded as speedily as a hunt, from a sound to a check, from a check to a view, from a view not to a death but hopefully to a new life. We were told by Ann Strawson that we transformed each other. We were flattered. Differences bound us together and we flourished in those early days which seemed they would never end. I don't remember a single disagreement.

We sliced through the next couple of months. It was no effort to fit in several hours of revision and new essays alongside being with Lisa. On many afternoons we were a domestic workshop at the top of the Oxford house. Lisa had decided to work for her exams. I worked for mine. Her column in *Cherwell* prospered.

In what was becoming a growing preoccupation, Lisa found her way into lino cuts. This apparently tame medium let loose a series of vivid images. Soon there were enough for a small exhibition which I organised in a spare room next to the Junior Common Room in Wadham. Michael, Ulick and Robert helped to carry the work through the streets – carefully shielded in brown paper – and each of them bought one of the lower-priced (£5 or £10) pictures. A positive *Cherwell* review was noticed by her friends at Ruskin. She was on her way!

Whenever there was time she came to see the films I would review – at least two a week. Her opinions were sometimes cutting but the French directors gave her great pleasure.

I looked up to her. Her opinions were so sophisticated, I thought. She saw in these films what I missed, teased out detail and developed it as a theme in the film. I thought she was brilliant. She was far cleverer than I was, all done with the flick of a phrase and in a foreign language. She was always uncompromising.

As a big treat we went to London to see *West Side Story*. I liked the idea of it: basing it on Shakespeare was so bold! And I thought the music was to be admired and also catchy. All this I had gathered from the reviews. We went to a Saturday matinée. I was swept away. Lisa shook her head. It was neither opera nor ballet, she argued, but a poor relative of both. It was commercial – not a word of praise in her haughty artistic vocabulary – and far too demotic. I enjoyed it. It was fresh, inventive, exciting and sexy. When I said that she just shook her head again.

Sometimes when I made what I thought were telling, even indisputable points, she found a way to cut me off at the knees. I loved the imminent smile when she put forward a contradiction; I enjoyed her pleasure in nailing an argument; I even enjoyed the rather grand manner in which she swept the whole of *West Side Story* aside. How dare she? But she did.

We waited in a bar at Paddington Station for a train back to Oxford. She told me, with quiet, moving passion, of the two operas to which her father had taken her. I remember that one was *Aida*. Such sacred events. Just her father and herself. Behind that story was so much longing, I thought at that time and think just as strongly now. Longing and emptiness. Presents brought back from his work abroad – he had laboratories in Brittany and Naples – but not always for her. She was so proud of the invitations he received to address scientific bodies and yet would jib at any mention of her parents' aristocratic or academic pedigrees. She had cut herself from all of that, she said and held to her decision. But what had replaced it? I was plain fare.

I remember, in that bar in Paddington Station, I lit up about the films of Ingmar Bergman. She had seen one only – *Smiles of a Summer Night*. The more we talked the more I realised that I was talking myself into a future. I had not the slightest notion of what I would try to do 'after Oxford'. But here it emerged: Lisa summed it up. She announced that I would be a film director! And write the films as well as direct them. Like Bergman . . . It was a wonderful madness in that bar in Paddington Station as Lisa took me seriously and made me feel that it was perfectly possible. She would paint. I would make films. Life was solved.

Chapter Twenty-four

I had soon abandoned the Elvis Presley look-a-like haircut and the official university photo portrays a neat and tidy crop not unlike that of everyone else. The age of the individual male peacock had not yet reached Oxford although I did buy a cheap black corduroy suit. The general uniform was not much of a variation on grey flannels, a workaday sports jacket and possibly a blazer. College ties and College scarves were thought stylish or naff depending on your rung on the ladder. Cavalry twill trousers were well up the ladder; cords a sturdy feature – deep brown most of all. Everything was a ladder. Starting with the degree ladder – Firsts, Seconds, Thirds, Passes; even the rooms allocated in college were a subtle ladder.

It was unsurprising that those with more got more – not that anyone save the half-witted was much bothered by that at the time, certainly not in Wadham, but it brought a touch of the past – the cravat was still a fancied throwback and on occasion something could be done with a coloured waistcoat. On the whole, though, we drifted unconsciously into a uniform not difficult or expensive to ape, and easy to tinker with. University garb was tailor-made for us. Like a pond for frogs we were in our own element. I suppose the hope was that, as in an Army training corps or a theological college, we would turn out to be much the same as others through the ages, clever enough, malleable, ready to serve.

There were rebels. In my time the most notable was Dennis Potter. On television I had seen a documentary he made about Oxford a year before I went to the university. For its day it was a bold broadside. He called it *The Glittering Coffin*, a title that described his thesis perfectly. I bumped into him two or three times, once memorably outside Trinity College. We were walking in opposite directions but he waved me to a halt and pronounced, in his ripe Forest of Dean tones:

'They say there's three real working-class men here. There's me. And you. Where's the other bugger?'

It was not true; the working class and more numerously what could be called the artisan class were nudging their way into Fortress Oxford with steadily increasing success. But Potter's observation had a smack of truth. The times were changing.

Ken Loach, the film director, was one of the great talents to emerge from Oxford at that time. He flowered in television and films. We were there at the same time but at university I knew him only as the actor I saw in a Restoration comedy.

His career as a left-wing film-maker whose work rocked the screen has spanned more than fifty years. Awards, congratulations, a devoted following, he is the prime example of Oxford helping to turn out someone whose expectations could not have been anywhere near the success he achieved. Like Dennis Potter, he found a way to mould the changing system to fit his ambitions. To do it so far from the 'Oxford Model' was remarkable. Much later I made a television programme about his work including his film on the Miners' Strike which was extremely difficult to place on a network apprehensive, with reason, about the reaction at the top of the system, which was determined to ban it. Working-class triumphalism was not supposed to seize the crown and become, as Ken Loach became, the outstanding English film-maker of his generation. From Evelyn Waugh to Ken Loach – in two generations!

Away from Oxford, the University of Hard Knocks was doing even better. Harold Pinter, who was to win the Nobel Prize for his plays, did not go to university. David Lean, the outstanding British film director, did not go to university. Laurence Olivier did not go to university – nor had Shakespeare, nor had Dickens, nor had Jane Austen, nor had the Beatles . . .

There are those who believe that universities are overvalued solely due to their antiquity, their mission to groom leaders in different areas of society. Yet for providing the introduction to guaranteed quality in the arts, the record of the universities was patchy, even feeble. Some thought that a university bled the genius out of an artist and someone like Evelyn Waugh survived and thrived so well because he ignored Oxford's basic examination expectations. And in the great arrival, the earthquake of contemporary 'pop' music which transformed the arts and music culture especially in America and the UK at the time, the universities scarcely figured at all. They were not designed for that. It is still relevant that what Oxford was best at was the past and the sciences and in turning out – a corps – who would manage and govern the rest of us.

There were positives. You could thrive on the liberty of the place. It was three years' leave from life as we would get to know it. But like all good things . . . We arrived at our final terms. Clearly ahead of us was the Reckoning: Finals. The word 'Final' was not attractive.

All of us took a few steps back for the Finals. Doomsday.

I wish I'd had the guts of Evelyn Waugh – to spend the three years, as he did, forging his character and his career. But it required a boldness and a confidence in the future that I lacked. Exams were there and they had to be taken because that is what people had to do. It was not a burden; it was the bill. You had been given the privilege of an Oxford education; you paid back by showing that the gift had been honoured. You had needed to pass exams to get into the place and, not too dissimilarly, you needed exams to get out of it. But of even greater importance was the Job. There had been, in the first year or two, the vague idea for most of us in the Wadham 1958 intake that Oxford would be a perfect maternity ward and deliver its new children into suitable occupations. The idea that these would have to be worked, even fought for, was not on the agenda. Oxford would deliver just by being Oxford.

There was a small office to which we were bidden and offered Opportunities. From big businesses to the civil service, from educational opportunities to Consett Iron and Steel Works. A form had to be filled in. I wanted to work in further education and filled in forms which would have transferred me to the Midlands. Advertising seemed a useful punt; that took me to an interview in Berkeley Square which led nowhere. But they flowed in, the offers for Oxford scalps. Companies would take over two or three rooms in one of the better hotels and we would shuffle in, be quizzed and shuffle out again, generally aware that it was no go.

Another World

There were hints that depending on the degree, which could turn out favourably, it might be a possibility for me to stay on and get a grant for a research project. Once explained, immediately rejected. To think of life continuing to be one of a daily immersion in research, forever chasing a thesis, offered no excitement.

Then the BBC came up. There were several categories you could apply for – the prize was the General Traineeship – of which three were offered each year. That was a two-year course sweeping you round the BBC, national, regional and international, radio and television. The man in the Opportunities office told me I had no chance but it wouldn't hurt to have a shot. Other universities would also be fielding their candidates so you never knew. I signed up but I also signed up for other BBC courses – one, studio manager for instance, a much safer bet, the man said. There would then be an interview process which was of great importance. I crossed my fingers for the Workers Education Authority project. It was also popular and well thought of. My job would begin as a junior tutor. I failed to get it.

I eventually got through to the last dozen or so of the Trainee Course and was called up to BBC Broadcasting House for the final interview for the General Traineeship.

My future was now in front of me. I was unprepared for it.

On the morning of the final BBC interview which was to be in London, I got to the railway station at Oxford and discovered I had nothing to read on the train. I bought a copy of *The Times* and read it end to end. At that stage I was used to speed-gutting articles. On the journey *The Times* had been swallowed whole. I had put on my three-piece suit. Bought in Carlisle three years ago, worn on special occasions, clerical grey, waistcoat, a white shirt, College tie, shoes polished front and back.

The Honourable Kenneth Lamb chaired the meeting. He gave me a kind look as I walked into the BBC room and faced the five interrogators. It was the kind of kind look, I thought later, that the executioner gives to the victim as he puts the noose around his neck. He leafed through my application. His conscientious attempt to put me at my ease made me uneasy.

I sensed that he wanted to get on with the next applicant as soon as possible. I sensed that the Honourable Kenneth had his own agenda.

He flicked through this and that: why had I given up rugby? Why had I chosen the Italian Renaissance as a special subject? Had Oxford been as I had anticipated from the viewpoint of a small northern town? Why the BBC? He skimmed through with laconic style and it seemed to me that I was not a runner.

Before he moved me on, he asked what was meant to be the 'killer' question. We'd been warned there was always one. What did I think of the current situation in Albania? For the first time I felt on top. I had read the article on Albania in that morning's *Times*. I had spent three years delivering summaries of such articles to the Oxford tutors and I rattled it off. He did not like it. He asked no more questions and immediately shuffled me off to interrogator number two, a flushed-faced, jolly-looking man in a pinstripe suit – from Personnel – who wanted to know more about 'this JACARI business'. He knew embarrassingly little about it and I had a free run. A question about what was new about Oxford – making a film and the Shakespeare trip down the Rhine which was carefully edited for the occasion. The attraction of the German audiences to our production went down well.

Finally a hitherto silent, glum-looking man wearing heavy spectacles came in with his question. This was Martin Esslin, a drama producer, one of the group of brilliant European intellectuals who were embraced by the World Service along with, among others, Konrad Syrop, Ludwig Gottlieb and Tosco Fyvel, who had worked with George Orwell. Martin had twinned his reputation on Radio Three with his work on Samuel Beckett, Joyce and Brecht, written books about their work and produced their work on radio. He had come very reluctantly to this board because at the last minute someone dropped out.

'What's the difference between Beckett and Joyce?' Had I been studying English, I might have had more of a chance. As it happened I had read both writers, though not as thoroughly as I feared Martin Esslin would want: most of all I had seen *Bloomsday*, a dashing dramatic recreation of James Joyce's *Ulysses*, adapted by Michael Kustow, another Wadham man, who was to dive into the metropolitan cultural world with an enormous splash. That was enough to give me a fingerhold. So I more or less held my own.

But that was not the best of it. Martin Esslin was intrigued by English working-class culture and the recent crop of novels, poems, plays and films which took that culture out of a lumpen proletariat backwater into the mainstream. He asked me if I wrote. I admitted – a bit. He then glanced (possibly for the first time!) at the notes I had sent in and flew into a discussion of why English working-class culture had been so unrepresented, why it was making so few inroads even now, what were the themes, what were my themes (much stumbling but graciously forgiven and augmented by Martin in fullest flow), and why was it so important to break the cultural class system. He was wonderful. Now and then I agreed or even added a sentence or so – enough it proved to quell into acquiescence the others around the table. I got in.

A month or so later, in the BBC canteen, Martin came across to me and said, 'Enjoying it here?'

'Yes. Yes! It's great.'

He beamed down at me. 'They didn't want you, you know. I had to fight my corner.' Then he waved. I can, truthfully, see him now, such a gentle wave, and the warmest smile. Martin Esslin changed my life.

* * *

The result of that interview did not emerge for a few weeks. That time was devoted to swotting. Finals began to roll into sight, dark clouds, outbreaks of hail and doubt, even thunder. For this surely was the Gunfight at the OK Corral. On this would be judged almost a decade of homework.

I had some catching up to do. Various digressions in the university years, especially Sarah, but more recently Lisa, had shrunk the time available for the solid slog that I saw as the only way to get what I wanted. I organised around Lisa's bed-sit and the College library. I felt too much under supervision to work in Mrs Prior's sitting room. Sometimes Ulick and I sat opposite each other and scribbled away, but it was never comfortable. I was used to an enwrapped and solitary silence, Ulick to the less rigorous but possibly more effective conversational approach. The conversation was either with me or with himself. 'Damn!' 'What a stupid question!' 'Who cares about Edward the Second?' 'Why were they so stupid about the Corn Laws?' As a fragmented running commentary, a sort of modern free verse history, it had its moments but not when I was struggling to make sense of the impact of Luther. So we went to the pub and later I stuck to one of the College libraries or to Lisa's artistic attic, now steadily filling up with her lino cuts.

Two days before Finals I felt ill; the following day I felt worse. Lawrence Stone directed me to a college doctor who said that I had glandular fever – which could be contagious – and ought to be isolated in a local hospital. Lawrence said that he would arrange for me an aegrotat, a sort of useless pass degree, which would enable me to stay on for another year with the same scholarship grants and with hints that good fortune could come from that. I could not bear the thought and insisted I was going to do the exams in hospital – all nine papers, taking up just over a week – and that I was not unhappy to do them from an isolation ward. The College was sympathetic. The hospital had a spare room. I went in with a stack of books and a change of clothes.

A supervisor – a vicar – was found who himself had had glandular fever and was now immune. He would arrive just before 9.30 a.m., hand me the examination paper and get down to the noisy business of reading the day's papers. I was comfortably propped up in bed, felt a little flaky and got on with it. The fever showed itself in small hard scarlet lumps which itched as badly as the rash of measles I'd had as a boy.

The advantages were the almost solitude, French windows opening on to a substantial and sunny lawn and the satisfaction of having got my own way to do the exams. The disadvantages were firstly the vicar, who had a passion for cocoa and nurses. Too often for me he would enquire whether I wanted a mug of cocoa. When I finally said yes to stop him asking again, there was great play in the summoning of the nurse – 'I hope it's our little dark-haired beauty!' – and the stirring of the mug. Not a task requiring much skill but the vicar made the most of it. The little red lumps made me sweat.

The other disadvantage was a young anaesthetist also presumably cleared of any contagious condition. He was a night owl. Those French windows in my room were open wide in the evening. It was a hot spell and the open window ushered in a slight breeze and sounds from the city, bells, distant roars from motorbikes.

The anaesthetist was always a bit tight. He took it for granted I would welcome him plonking himself on the bedside chair at about nine o'clock when I was just finishing the final run-through for the next day's exams. He always wanted to discuss the Great Questions: was there a God? What had come before the stars? Should we have gone to battle over the Suez Canal? He was polite but insistent and I was too feeble to ask him to push off.

A day before the final paper, which would be to translate a passage from Latin and two contemporary European languages into English and put a segment of English into Latin, I was told that I could leave in a couple of days. The mass of hard scarlet bumps was receding. The doctor was now prepared to come near and chat. He even looked over my shoulder at the passages in Italian and hummed them to himself.

When he left and I had eaten the lunch provided, I went to the bathroom, had a shower, put on the spare clothes I had brought along and decided to leave. It was the last day. My examinations were done.

It was a hot summer's day. I went out on to the broad lawn, hugged the shade provided by buildings, got to the main gate and I was free!

From there it was a haul. Over Magdalen Bridge, remembering the last May morning when Ulick, Robert and myself had done what undergraduates are supposed to do – hired a punt at five in the morning, manoeuvred it downriver, to jostle similar punts peopled by similar undergraduates who were following a similar tradition to reach Magdalen Tower at dawn and listen to the choir singing in the new season. We had taken two bottles of wine and packets of biscuits. It was as if we had to do it because others had done it for centuries and this was therefore what you did. Your role was to keep the tradition going and make yourself enjoy it. There was quite a bit of that at Oxford.

From there, up Longwall Street, I walked alongside Magdalen College Deer Park, always seeking shade as the rising heat and the watery legs weakened an already enfeebled body. I swung into Parks Road, was tempted by the yells and cheers coming from Wadham College as the liberated celebrated. But I reckoned I had just about enough puff to get to Lisa's flat. Past Keble College – more whoops and cheers – across the Banbury Road and the Woodstock Road, both littered with rather tipsy undergraduates still in the outfit – white tie, dark suit, black gown – which was the examination uniform, once again behaving as if a siege had been lifted. Finally there, at the Strawsons' door, the bell, the entrance, the flights of stairs. I dropped on to the bed soaked in sweat and slept as if I had passed out and woke to a pot of tea, a bowl of vegetable soup and bread. I had a cigarette and went back to sleep.

I remembered to ask Lisa to contact Ulick, to tell Mrs Prior I was convalescing within the rules.

Chapter Twenty-five

There was little approval. There were polite nods in that direction but they were outnumbered by the negatives – those openly expressed and those it was easy to read in the expressions. 'Rather foolish' was one of the kinder remarks. 'Far too young' was another. 'A classic mismatch' and 'Why don't they just have an affair?'

An affair was never contemplated. Perhaps the world of Lisa might have tolerated it but to me it seemed too foreign. You 'went' with someone with the intention, however near or far in the future, of marrying them. Or you used a pregnancy as a gun to the head and that was that. 'Going' with someone could be protracted. There was a man in Wigton, a cobbler, who 'went' with his fiancée for fourteen years. They walked from the church the mile to the Red Dial pub every Sunday night following evensong. Eventually they spliced, moved in together and ceased the Sunday walks. An affair suggested something flighty, unsubstantial, foreign, built on shifting sands. We came somewhere near the 'love at first sight' category. But it was the practical considerations that clinched us.

Whatever happened, if the BBC came through, I would be leaving Oxford, most likely for London. Lisa was adhesively fixed to Oxford. It had the ambience of dedicated scholarship which her father had passed on to her. She had now struck out into a new direction on her own terms and it was working – the exhibition had been successful enough and this time she had sailed through the exams. She could stay on at the Ruskin Art School as she – or rather her father – paid her way or . . . find another niche in Oxford. She had the Strawsons' flat as a refuge, friends at the art school for company and now the regular article in *Cherwell* which gave her a routine and a place in the university's scheme of things.

If I went to London to work, which would surely be the destiny of any job I went to, and continued to live in Oxford as, after the briefest of exploratory discussions, was her much preferred option, there would be the daily trek. I reckoned about two hours each way. It was such a waste of time. And why not give London a go? If it backfired we could always return to Oxford. Lisa was reassured by that but far from excited at the prospect of London. One transplant, Paris–Oxford, was enough. But she said that if she had to go to London, she would, foreign though it was. It was a sacrifice.

Almost as a farewell tour we walked through the parks and along the river. We pottered around the riddled streets of central Oxford. We took a punt and made it downriver without too much embarrassment. We met her friends. She met mine. They were good encounters with Lisa in her element in this amiable intellectual chat. We went to see films and plays; we had as easy and enjoyable life as we had ever had in Oxford. This was what life was supposed to be like.

* * *

The marriage ceremony was held in the Town Hall. There is a lovely photograph of Lisa coming out – so fresh, smiling, her hair 'done', which I'd never seen before, framing a face full of hesitant joy.

Her father had visited Oxford a few times and made it his business over his two-day visit to call on scholars with whom he had corresponded. Lisa's pride in him glowed. He was portly, a sweet smile, sweet temper, hugely grateful to the Strawsons and pleased to meet everyone, especially gallant to my mother who, having discovered we had no wedding cake, had found a shop in the market and carried the cake throughout the service.

It was sliced in Wadham Gardens under the great copper beech tree where we had a brief party. Ulick, the best man, delivered a short speech – his girlfriend Eileen, the 'corker', made an immediate friendship with Lisa. Michael poured the drinks. Lawrence Stone was accidentally strolling in the garden and joined in, and soon engaged with my father. It went like a blink. We had packed that morning. Our cases were in the Lodge. We walked to the bus station and went for our three-day-two-night honeymoon at Witney. At some time late in the day, Lisa's stepmother, who had collared me ostensibly for lunch but for what proved to be an interrogation, reported back to Lisa that I was too young for her and it was very unlikely to last. Lisa told me this on the bus and tried to laugh it off.

We walked most of the day and read to each other in the evenings.

Chapter Twenty-six

A couple of days after we came back to Oxford, I went to Wadham to collect my post.

The BBC had taken me on. Could I get in touch with them about a starting date. The middle of January would be ideal, to meet at Broadcasting House, Portland Place, at 9.30 a.m.: the salary would be £620 a year. Congratulations. I put the letter in my inside pocket and saved it for the right moment with Lisa. I was cock-a-hoop.

* * *

The other letter was from Sarah. My hands shook, just a little, but indisputably they shook as I pushed my thumb into the envelope and untidily ripped it open.

> Dear Melvyn,
> I just heard this morning that you had got married. Congratulations! They say she is French and an artist. Funnily enough I am getting married soon. He's called Juan. He's Spanish. He came to work in a hotel in the Lake District to get experience – his brothers own a big place in Barcelona and they want to attract more English customers. An acquaintance of theirs has this hotel just outside of Keswick. We met up in Keswick itself and got on. He came to Wigton where he's working in Mason's Garage to earn some ready money

before he goes back. He's asked me to go with him and I've said I would. You would like him.

This is awkward and I'm sorry but do you mind if I ask you whether you had met Lisa before you and I split up? One way and another it would help to know.

I saw your mam yesterday. She seems a bit taken aback, but I'm sure she'll take it in her stride.

Wigton doesn't change.

With warmest wishes

Sarah

P.S. I'm learning Spanish.

* * *

Dear Sarah,

Got your letter. Congratulations to you, as well.

Things are going well here. I've got a job at the BBC. Lisa had an exhibition. Michael and Ulick were there. Alan is working in London and Robert has taken off for Edinburgh.

Your question. No. I had not set eyes on Lisa before we broke up. In fact it's because we broke up that I set eyes on her in the first place! Someone invited me to a party and there she was. So you could say that it was because of what you did that I met her!

We'll be going to Brittany for a week or two. Her father is a scientist and he has the use of a laboratory there. Then we'll be flat-hunting in London. Another life.

I hope you and Juan do well. I only know Barcelona because of George Orwell. I looked it up and it seems like a great place. Good luck to both of you.

With all good wishes, and good luck.

Melvyn

* * *

There was a note from Lawrence Stone. 'Could you drop in and see me? About six o'clock.'

For what would be the last time I spiralled up the narrow staircase to that perfect academic room which had seen so much scientific scholarship as well as centuries of undergraduates ploughing through their essays.

Lawrence as usual was dug into an armchair, notes scattered around his feet. Despite these impediments, he stood up.

'A very good Second,' he said. 'Despite everything. Well done!' We pumped out a handshake. 'Sherry?'

I had come to loathe sherry.

'Thank you.'

He held up his glass. So did I. We sipped.

'You might like to consider staying on.'

'With a Second?'

'It's not unusual. Your friend Peter Strawson, one of our best philosophers, took a Second. I am suggesting you may like to consider it.'

I took my time. The thought of being buried in books forever after . . . The offer from the BBC was burning a hole in my pocket.

'I've been offered a job at the BBC. Well, a traineeship.'

'I've heard about those.' Lawrence smiled. 'Possibly more "exciting",' he said. 'You could always come back here later. Good luck.'

And again we raised our neat sherry glasses and again we sipped.

'Keep in touch,' he said. 'I was rather looking forward to you digging up more about your Celtic saints from the north.' He smiled. 'I think that was the longest and I might add the most enthusiastic essay I sat through! I thought that you would be the man to bring it into the field.'

For a moment . . . for a flickering moment . . .

* * *

Lisa and I went to Concarneau where her stepmother's dowry had paid for a chalet in the woods just a few score yards from the shoreline.

We watched the fishing boats come in at evening. We went into the labyrinth of small back streets which knotted together the old town. We ate French pancakes. Lisa got to know the local painter who had been to the École des Beaux-Arts in the middle of Paris near the Sorbonne. We played boules. I got badly sunburnt, to the embarrassment of Lisa, like a typical British working-class tourist, white skin seduced by the sun. Lisa and her brother collected small shells on the seashore which she put in a large specimen bottle her father let her take from his laboratory. We saw the marching bands of all the surrounding fishing villages in the Festival des Filets Bleus.

We took a small boat and went sailing, out beyond the old port, out to sea, just the two of us, tempting the land to disappear, reckless, fearless, full of hope.

The End

London
July 2025

Acknowledgements

My cousin Geoffrey Hocking was extremely helpful, for the paragraphs about Fletchertown.

The booklets by Mick James and the people of Fletchertown were a detailed revelation of coal mining there and provided much other local information so carefully gathered.

I owe a great deal to the friendships established in Wadham College and especial thanks to Jane Garnett for her close reading of the book. Many thanks also go to Charlotte Humphery at Sceptre.

Caroline Michel's help and guidance were invaluable.

My wife Gabriel has been indispensable in what proved to be a protracted editing process.

Finally I want to remember Joan Martos who – as Sarah – is key to this book but alas died before it was published.

RAISING READERS
Books Build Bright Futures

Dear Reader,

We'd love your attention for one more page to tell you about the crisis in children's reading, and what we can all do.

Studies have shown that reading for fun is the **single biggest predictor of a child's future life chances** – more than family circumstance, parents' educational background or income. It improves academic results, mental health, wealth, communication skills, ambition and happiness.[1]

The number of children reading for fun is in rapid decline. Young people have a lot of competition for their time. In 2024, 1 in 10 children and young people in the UK aged 5 to 18 did not own a single book at home.[2]

Hachette works extensively with schools, libraries and literacy charities, but here are some ways we can all raise more readers:

- Reading to children for just 10 minutes a day makes a difference
- Don't give up if children aren't regular readers – there will be books for them!
- Visit bookshops and libraries to get recommendations
- Encourage them to listen to audiobooks
- Support school libraries
- Give books as gifts

There's a lot more information about how to encourage children to read on our website: **www.RaisingReaders.co.uk**

Thank you for reading.

---

[1] OECD, '21st-Century Readers: Developing Literacy Skills in a Digital World', 2021, https://www.oecd.org/en/publications/21st-century-readers_a83d84cb-en.html

[2] National Literacy Trust, 'Book Ownership in 2024', November 2024, https://literacytrust.org.uk/research-services/research-reports/book-ownership-in-2024